## "I'm Grant Hardesty, volunteer d

The woman's
seemed made
cool reserve v
Maggie Davi

"Nice to meet you, Maggie." It hadn't been so far, but things might improve.

Maggie lifted the envelope she held. "Your paperwork arrived the same day you did, Doctor. That's the way the mail usually functions up here in the mountains. I didn't think they'd send us a new doctor until after the holidays."

"You got lucky," he said lightly.

"Yes." She looked him over. "Now that you've seen what Button Gap is like, do you still intend to stay?"

There was a challenge in the words that he didn't miss. For whatever reason, Maggie Davis either didn't want him to stay or didn't think he would. Or maybe both.

He lifted an eyebrow, smiling slightly. "Sorry to disappoint you, Ms. Davis. I fully intend to stay."

## Books by Marta Perry

Love Inspired

*Hunter's Bride
*A Mother's Wish
*A Time to Forgive
*Promise Forever
  Always in Her Heart
  The Doctor's Christmas
  True Devotion
†Hero in Her Heart
†Unlikely Hero
†Hero Dad
†Her Only Hero
†Hearts Afire
†Restless Hearts
†A Soldier's Heart
  Mission: Motherhood
**Twice in a Lifetime
**Heart of the Matter
**The Guardian's Honor
**Mistletoe Prayers
  "The Bodine Family Christmas"
  Her Surprise Sister

Love Inspired Suspense

*Tangled Memories
  Season of Secrets
††Hide in Plain Sight
††A Christmas to Die For
††Buried Sins
  Final Justice
  Twin Targets

*Caldwell Kin
†The Flanagans
**The Bodine Family
††The Three Sisters Inn

## MARTA PERRY

has written everything from Sunday-school curricula to travel articles to magazine stories in more than twenty years of writing, but she feels she's found her writing home in the stories she writes for the Love Inspired lines.

Marta lives in rural Pennsylvania, but she and her husband spend part of each year at their second home in South Carolina. When she's not writing, she's probably visiting her children and her six beautiful grandchildren, traveling, gardening or relaxing with a good book.

Marta loves hearing from readers, and she'll write back with a signed bookmark and/or her brochure of Pennsylvania Dutch recipes. Write to her c/o Love Inspired Books, 233 Broadway, Suite 1001, New York, NY 10279, email her at marta@martaperry.com, or visit her on the web at www.martaperry.com.

# The Doctor's Christmas

## Marta Perry

*Love Inspired*

Recycling programs
for this product may
not exist in your area.

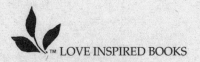 ™ LOVE INSPIRED BOOKS

ISBN-13: 978-0-373-78734-0

THE DOCTOR'S CHRISTMAS

Copyright © 2003 by Martha Johnson

www.LoveInspiredBooks.com

Printed in U.S.A.

Worship and serve God with your whole heart and a willing mind. For the Lord sees every heart and understands and knows every plan and thought.
—*1 Chronicles* 28:9

This story is dedicated to Bjoern Jacob,
Greta Nicole and Ameline Grace,
with love from Grammy.

And, as always, to Brian.

# Chapter One

Grant Hardesty strode into the clinic's waiting room.
Empty and quiet, until a child's wail issued from an
exam room beyond the counter. He tossed his jacket
onto a chair. Whether he wanted it to or not, his stint as
a volunteer doctor at the isolated mountain clinic was
apparently starting right now.

The exam room door stood open. A kid of about nine
or ten sat crying on the table, while his mother stood
next to him, wringing her hands. A woman who must
be the clinic's nurse struggled to pull the boy's hands
away from the cut on his face without knocking over
the suture tray.

He gave a cursory knock on the door frame, barely
breaking his stride. "I'm Grant Hardesty. It looks as if
you have a patient for me already." He headed for the
sink, folding back his sleeves with a nod to the nurse.
"I'll do the suturing. You settle him down."

The woman swung toward him, moving in front of

the child protectively. "What are you talking about? Who are you?"

Grant did a quick assessment. Jeans, boots, a flannel shirt over a white tee. What had happened to lab coats and name badges? The woman had thick glossy dark hair, short and straight, a pair of startled dark eyes and a stubborn chin. She did not look welcoming.

"I'm Dr. Hardesty," he repeated. He started to take her place next to the patient, but she didn't move. "From Volunteer Doctors. They must have informed you I was coming."

The surprise in her face told him the answer to that one. She hadn't expected him. Some bureaucrat must have fouled up.

The woman's surprise was accompanied by something else. Before he could analyze what, the kid wailed again, the mother echoing his cry.

"Look, we'll have a welcoming ceremony later. Let's get the patient taken care of first."

He didn't have to analyze her reaction to that suggestion. Anger and indignation battled for supremacy.

"If you think I'll turn my patient over to you without knowing more than that, you must be crazy." Western Maryland accents were softer, lazier than Baltimorese, but hers had sharpened with anger.

The mother stifled a sob. "Maggie, if he's a doctor—"

"We don't know that." She darted an annoyed glance at the woman. "Somebody walks in off the street and you want him to treat Tommy without knowing a thing about him just because he claims to be a doctor? I don't think so."

Maybe he should appreciate her caution, but he just wanted to cross off one day from his sentence here. Grant yanked his hospital ID from his pocket and tossed it to her. "Grant Hardesty, M.D. Okay?"

She let go of the kid to catch it, and the boy made a determined lunge to escape. Grant caught him, plopping him back on the table and getting a kick in the stomach for his trouble.

He clenched his teeth to keep back a groan. "Satisfied? Let's get this done. I repeat. You hold, I suture."

She frowned at his ID for another moment, then gave in with a reluctant nod.

"Gloves are on the tray." She took the kid's hands. "Come on, Tommy. The new doctor will take good care of you."

She probably didn't actually mean that reassurance, but at least she seemed done arguing.

He snapped on the gloves and checked the tray. He'd dealt with antagonistic medical personnel before. He could handle this one, even if she did dress more like a female lumberjack than a nurse.

He sensed her gaze assessing his every move even as she talked to the kid, distracting him while Grant cleaned up the boy's forehead. The cut was nothing too drastic—no doubt she could have handled it herself, but that was why he was here. Wasn't it?

He half listened to her chiding the kid about crossing

some creek on a log. He'd committed himself to tending the medical needs of this western Maryland mountain county for the next month. It wasn't what he'd intended to do after completing his residency, but the eventual reward would be worthwhile.

So here he was, lost in the wilderness until Christmas. He suppressed the edge that always entered his mind at the thought of the holiday.

At least, this job would get him away from his mother's round of society parties. That was something to appreciate, anyway.

The boy had stopped wiggling, listening intently as— what had the mother called her? Maggie, that was it—as Maggie told him a story about encountering a bear in the woods. Fanciful, but it kept him quiet.

"There you are." He stood back, pleased with the neat stitches. He hadn't lost his touch. "The nurse will give you a sheet of follow-up instructions."

He went to the sink to wash up. Before he treated any more patients, he'd get a lab coat out of his bag. It didn't look as if he could count on the free clinic to provide them.

He heard the soft murmur of the nurse's voice as she took mother and son to the outer office, explaining the instructions to the mother. Nurse Maggie seemed to have all the kindness in the world for her patients. And none for him.

Well, that was too bad. Presumably she was used to working with different doctors, since they rotated in and out of this place. She'd just have to adjust to his way of doing things.

If he stayed. The thought that had recurred since he left Baltimore came again. He didn't have to stay.

The outer door had closed. He went back to the reception area, noticing pale green walls that needed a new paint job, posters urging flu shots and well-baby checkups, a row of metal folding chairs. Maggie whatever-her-name-was stood at the desk in the little cubbyhole behind the counter, frowning down at an envelope in her hand.

"Let's start over again." He leaned against the doorjamb, giving her what he hoped was a friendly smile. "I'm Grant Hardesty, volunteer doctor of the month."

The woman's chocolate-colored eyes seemed made for smiling, but they held a cool reserve when she looked at him. "I'm Maggie Davis. *Permanent* nurse." She laid a faint stress on the word.

"Nice to meet you, Maggie." It hadn't been so far, but things might improve. He slid his jacket back on.

She lifted the envelope she held. "Your paperwork arrived the same day you did, Doctor. That's the way the mail usually functions up here in the mountains. I didn't think they'd send us a new doctor until after the holidays."

"You got lucky," he said lightly.

"Yes." She looked him over, seeming to estimate the cost of his leather jacket and Italian loafers. "Now that you've seen what Button Gap is like, do you still intend to stay?"

There was a challenge in the words that he didn't miss. For whatever reason, Maggie Davis either didn't want him to stay or didn't think he would. Or maybe both.

Well, she was wrong. With faint surprise, he realized that at some point in the past half hour, he'd made a decision.

He lifted an eyebrow, smiling slightly. "Sorry to disappoint you, Ms. Davis. I fully intend to stay."

In her need to get rid of him, she'd given herself away. Maggie gritted her teeth. She should at least pretend to be welcoming.

"I'm not disappointed. It's just that the last volunteer doctor they sent us from the city couldn't make it twenty-four hours without his mocha lattes."

His eyes, as changeably blue and green as Elk Lake, narrowed a little at the implied criticism. His eyebrow quirked in a question. "Does that mean people will be taking chances on how long I'll stay?"

The county board that ran the clinic would undoubtedly not appreciate her antagonizing the new doctor the first hour he was here. She tried to smile.

"It won't be that bad. But outsiders do sometimes find staying in Button Gap a bit of a culture shock."

"I'm here to provide medical services, not run for citizen of the year." He abandoned the casual posture, straightening to an imposing six feet or so. The height went well with his classic, even features, his expensively cut brown hair and the tilt of his head that seemed to say he was better than everyone else.

She stiffened her spine. Aunt Elly would call him a "fine figure of a man," no doubt. Well, Aunt Elly didn't have to work with him.

"No, they won't elect you citizen of the year," she said. "But they'll probably arrive bearing welcoming casseroles."

"I'll have to count on you to tell me how to respond, won't I?" He gestured toward the doorway. "For now, you can give me the grand tour."

She nodded, moving reluctantly past him, getting a whiff of some expensive, musky aftershave. She knew his type. She'd certainly seen it enough times. Dr. Grant Hardesty was your typical doctor-on-the-way-up, filled with the arrogance that came from an expensive education, a doting family and a hospital staff who'd probably catered to his every whim.

She was stuck with him for the next month, and he couldn't have come at a worse time. A fleeting surge of panic touched her, and she beat it back down. She didn't panic.

In spite of the determined set to the man's firm mouth, she doubted he'd last a week, let alone a month. He probably had an elegant girlfriend back in Baltimore and a list of holiday parties a mile long. She'd just make sure he didn't tumble onto her secret in the meantime.

"You've already seen our exam room." She started down the hall.

He stopped her with a light touch on the arm. "Room, singular?"

The criticism in his voice annoyed her all over again. "One exam room." The words were crisp. "One waiting room. One nurse/secretary/receptionist. This is a free clinic, not Johns Hopkins. We're lucky the county provides the building and my salary."

He lifted his hands. "Okay, truce. I was just surprised. I know you serve most of the county."

She nodded. At least he realized how big this job was. "Lots of miles, but not so many people. Not enough, anyway, to convince a doctor to stay full-time since old Doc Harriman died, and that was fifteen years ago."

She gestured toward the door they passed. "That's locked storage. We have to keep meds on hand, because the nearest pharmacy is twenty miles away."

He frowned, absorbing that information. "Where do you take patients if it's something we can't handle here?"

"Hagerstown has the closest hospital, and that's a good forty miles. They have a Life Flight chopper they can bring in, unless the weather's bad."

"You make Button Gap sound like the last frontier."

"Maybe it is, when it comes to medical care, anyway."

He wouldn't appreciate the significance of that. How could he? Someone like Grant Hardesty couldn't understand either the terrifying challenge or the immense satisfaction of providing the only medical care some of Button Gap's residents would ever have.

They reached the end of the hall. "The office." She swung the door open. "You can use it, but some of the patient files and insurance forms are stored in here, so I'm in and out all the time."

She'd found it best to make that clear right away with the visiting doctors. Otherwise, they'd assume it was their private sanctuary.

He glanced dismissively at the tiny room with its battered oak desk, flea-market chairs and office-supply-overstock file cabinets. "It'll do."

"The clinic's hours are over for the day, so if you want to get settled—"

She left it open-ended, wondering how he'd respond. He so clearly didn't want to be here that she couldn't imagine why he'd volunteered to come in the first place. Maybe he'd thought it would be a nice addition to his résumé.

He just nodded. "My bags are outside."

Apparently he intended to give the clinic a try. At any other time, she'd be grateful. But now—

She spared a fleeting thought for Aunt Elly, who'd taken over for her at home when she'd had to rush into the clinic.

The elderly woman hadn't lost any of the loving spunk that had once made her the perfect foster mother for a scared, defiant eleven-year-old. She'd be all right until Maggie could get back to take over.

"I'll help you bring your things in and show you the apartment."

She led the way outside, wondering what he saw when he looked at Button Gap. The village was only a few hours' drive from his busy hospital in Baltimore, but to him it probably looked as if it had not changed for the past century.

White frame houses and a couple of log cabins clustered around a village center composed of a general store and café, the post office with a flag flying in the wind and the medical clinic. White picket fences enclosed neat front gardens, their late chrysanthemums killed by the last frost. The heavily forested mountain ridges surrounded the town on all sides, rearing upward to cut off the gray November sky.

Maggie looked at it and saw home. He probably saw a hamlet with no coffee bar or decent restaurant in sight.

She might have predicted the new SUV he drove. It had probably been shiny clean when he left the city, but miles of mountain road had splashed it with mud.

He opened the back, and she grabbed the nearest duffel while he picked up two other bags. They matched, of course.

She nodded toward the long frame building that had been first a private home and then a grocery store before the county bought it for the clinic.

"The apartment for visiting doctors is on that side of the office. Mine is on the other side."

He sent a cursory glance from one to the other. "Okay." He took a computer bag from the front seat and slammed the vehicle's door, locking it with an electronic key. "Let's have a look."

She unlocked the apartment's front door and ushered him in, trying not to smile as he glanced around the living room. The county had been cheap with the furnishings, figuring none of the volunteers stayed long enough to make it worth fixing up the place. The beige carpet, brown couch, faux leather recliner and small television on a fake wood stand gave it the air of a motel room.

"The kitchen's through here, bedroom and bath there."

He took it in with a comprehensive glance. "I trust your place is a little better than this, since you're the *permanent* staff." His stress on the word said he hadn't missed her earlier dig.

"Mine was the living room and kitchen in the original house, so it has a bit more charm." She dropped the bag she'd carried in. "This part was once a grocery store. They knocked down the shelving and put in the kitchen to make it livable."

His expression suggested he didn't find it particularly livable. "Is it always this cold?"

"The county can't afford to heat the place when no one's here." She indicated the cellar door. "I'll start the furnace, but you'd better come with me to see how it works, just in case it shuts off on you in the middle of the night."

She'd prefer he not think she was at his beck and call for household emergencies.

Taking the flashlight from its hook, she opened the door, letting out a damp smell. She vividly recalled the female doctor who'd flatly refused to go into the cellar at all. Grant looked as if he were made of sterner stuff than that, but you never could tell.

She took a steadying breath and led the way down the rickety wooden stairs. Truth to tell, she hated dark, damp places herself. But she wouldn't give in to that fear, not anymore.

Grant's footsteps thudded behind her. He had to duck his head to avoid a low beam, and he seemed too close in the small space.

"There's the monster." She flicked the light on the furnace—a squat, ugly, temperamental beast. "It's oil fired, but the motor's electric."

She checked the oil gauge, knelt next to the motor and flipped the switch. Nothing.

Grant squatted next to her, putting one hand on her shoulder to steady himself as he repeated her action. His touch was warm and strong, giving her the ridiculous desire to lean against him.

"Doesn't sound too promising."

His voice was amused, rather than annoyed, as if he'd decided laughter was the best way of handling the situation. Maybe he was imagining the stories he'd have to tell, back in the city, about his sojourn in the wilderness.

"It's just stubborn." She stood, putting a little distance between them. She closed the door that covered the switch, then gave it a hearty kick. The furnace coughed, grumbled and started to run.

"Nice technique," he said. "I'll remember that." His voice was low and rich with amusement, seeming to touch a chord within her that hadn't been touched in a long time.

She swung around, the beam of the flashlight glancing off rickety wooden shelves lined with dusty canning jars. A wave of discomfort hit her, and she went quickly to the stairs.

"The furnace will keep running until the thermostat clicks off, but it's always a little drafty upstairs. I hope you brought a few sweaters." *I hope you decide this isn't for you.*

If he left, they'd be without a doctor until after the holidays. If he stayed—

She didn't have any illusions about his reaction if he discovered the secret she hid. No one else in Button Gap would give her away, but he might.

"I'll make do," he said. He closed the cellar door behind them.

Grant wouldn't have a chance to give her away, because he'd never know. She'd make sure of that.

"Do you have a family, Maggie?"

Her heart stopped. "No. Why do you ask?"

His gaze fixed on her face, frowning, as if he considered a diagnosis. "I thought I saw a kid at your window when I arrived."

"That must have been Callie." She tried for a light laugh. "My cat. She loves to sit in the window and watch the birds. You probably saw her."

He gave her a cool, superior look that said he wasn't convinced. "Must have been, I guess."

*Oh, Lord, I'm sorry. Really I am. But isn't protecting some of Your little ones worth a white lie?*

Somehow she didn't think God weighed sins the way she'd like Him to.

And she also had a sinking feeling that told her she might not get rid of Grant Hardesty anytime soon.

"So you lied to the man, child?" Aunt Elly looked up from the piecrust she was rolling out on Maggie's kitchen table, her faded blue eyes shrewd behind her steel-rimmed glasses.

"I didn't want to." The defensive note in her voice made her sound eleven again, trying every trick in the foster-kid book on Aunt Elly before realizing the woman knew them all and loved her anyway. "But I didn't want him to find out about the Bascoms."

She shot a glance toward the living room, where Tacey, five, and Robby, four, were playing some kind of a game. Joey, at eight considering himself the man of the family, wasn't in her line of sight. He'd probably curled up with a book on the couch, keeping an eye on his siblings. She lowered her voice.

"You don't know what he's like. Stiff-necked, by-the-book and arrogant to boot. I can't take the risk of letting him know about the kids. He's the type to call social services the minute he knew."

Aunt Elly fitted the top crust over apple slices from her own McIntosh tree. "So you been saying, child. But you don't know that for sure. Might be good to have a doctor handy with three rambunctious kids in the house."

"I can take care of them. Besides, Nella will be

back soon." She wouldn't give in to the fear that Nella Bascom, having lived with an abusive husband for too many years, just didn't have it in her to raise her kids alone.

"You heard anything more from her?" Aunt Elly slid the pie into the oven and closed the door.

"Three cards and one phone call." She nodded at the Christmas card she'd taped on the refrigerator where the children could see it every day. "She says she'll be back for Christmas. That's what she said in the note she left with the kids in the office."

Shock had hit her when she'd opened the office that morning and found the Bascom kids in the waiting room. Tacey and Robby had been curled up like a pair of kittens, sleeping since Nella had left them at dawn. Joey had been watching over them.

"Nella will come back," she said again firmly, as if Aunt Elly had argued with her. "Once she gets used to the idea that her husband isn't around to hurt her anymore, she'll adjust."

"You could go looking for her."

She could. The postmarks told her Nella had run to the small West Virginia town where she'd once lived. "I've thought about it. Prayed about it. But—"

Aunt Elly nodded. "You figure if Nella's going to have strength enough to raise those youngsters on her own, she'd best come back on her own."

"She will. And I'm not going to let those kids get sucked into the system in the meantime. Nella would probably never get them back if that happened."

They both knew what Maggie had experienced in the foster care system. It lay unspoken between them.

"I reckon Button Gap can take care of its own," Aunt Elly said. She glanced out the kitchen window. "But it looks like you'll have to tell the new doc something."

"Why?" She slid off her stool, dusting her hands on her jeans.

"'Cause here he comes, and he's got ahold of Joey by the collar."

Before Maggie could move, a knock thundered at the door. Shooting Aunt Elly an appalled look, she moved to open it.

Grant stood on her step, holding Joey by his frayed jacket collar. "This kid belong to you?"

"Not exactly." She grabbed the boy, pulling him inside the kitchen. "He's a friend. What are you doing with him?"

"I found him in the cellar." He stepped inside without waiting for an invitation. "He was trying to dismantle my furnace."

"He can't have been." Her rejection was automatic, but her heart sank. Actually, he could. Joey was fascinated by all things mechanical. Worse, he might have heard her earlier and decided to help the new doctor go away.

"Yes, he was." Grant planted his hands on his hips, glowering at her. Then he seemed to become aware of Aunt Elly, watching him with what might have been an appreciative twinkle in her eyes. And of Tacey and

Robby, standing in the doorway, looking scared. "Sorry, I didn't realize you had company."

"Not company." Aunt Elly wiped her hand on the sprigged apron she wore over a faded housedress, then extended it to him. "I'm Aunt Elly. I guess you're the new doctor."

"Grant Hardesty." He sent Maggie an annoyed glance. "I thought you said you didn't have any family. Your aunt—"

"Nope, not her aunt." Aunt Elly was obviously enjoying herself. "Ellenora Glenning, if you want to be formal."

"Mrs. Glenning—" he began.

"Call me Aunt Elly," she said. "Everyone does." She grabbed her bulky gray sweater from the coat hook inside the door. "I'd better get, Maggie. Watch that pie. And you children behave yourselves, you hear?" She twinkled at Grant. "You two can probably fight better without me here."

She scooted out the door, leaving Maggie to face the music.

Maggie gave Joey a gentle push toward the living room. "You go in and play a game with your brother and sister now. We'll talk about this later."

Joey sent a sidelong look at Grant. "I won't be far off, if you need me."

She tousled his fine blond hair. "I know. Go on, now."

When he and the other children were out of sight, she turned back to Grant.

"Why did you lie to me?" he asked before she had time to think.

"I didn't, not exactly." Well, that sounded feeble. "You asked if I had any family. I don't." She pointed to the windowsill where the elderly calico cat slept, oblivious to the hubbub. "And you might have seen Callie."

"I might have, but I didn't." His frown deepened. "It's obvious these kids are staying with you. Why didn't you want me to know?"

Part of the truth was better than none. "Their mother is a friend of mine. She had to go out of town for a few days, so I'm watching them while she's gone."

"That doesn't explain why you didn't tell me the truth when I asked."

"Look, I just didn't want you to think the children would interfere with my work." She hated saying it, hated sounding as if he had the right to disapprove of anything she did. "They won't. I have plenty of people to take care of them when I'm working."

"Your system didn't seem to work too well when the boy decided to take my furnace apart."

"Joey. His name is Joey." She took a breath. He had a point, unfortunately. "I'm sorry about that. He's interested in how things work. Do you need me to come over and fix it?"

"I can manage." There was a note to his voice that she didn't like. "But I don't want to work with someone I can't trust."

She wanted to lash out at him, tell him she didn't want to work with him, either. Tell him to take his changeable eyes and his chiseled profile and go right back to Baltimore where he belonged.

But she couldn't. Like it or not, she was stuck with him.

## Chapter Two

Maybe he shouldn't have been that rough on her. Maggie's face looked pale and stiff, her promise delivered through set lips. They'd definitely gotten off on the wrong foot, mostly her fault, but he didn't need to contribute to it.

Not being told the truth was a flash point with him, maybe because his parents had spent so much of their time either avoiding the truth or prettying it up until it became palatable to them.

Still, he had to work with the woman for the next month, and he was the temporary, not she. He needed to establish normal business relations with her, or his time here would be even more difficult.

He forced a smile. "Look, we've had a rocky beginning. What do you say we start over?"

Emotions flitted rapidly across her face. Maggie wasn't as impassive as she probably liked to believe. He could see her questioning his motives and wondering whether he meant what he said. He could see her distaste at the thought of cooperating with him. And then he saw her reluctant acceptance.

Why reluctant? What made her tick? His own curiosity surprised him.

She tilted her head, considering. "Maybe that would be best." She took a deep breath, as if preparing to plunge into cold water. "Welcome to Button Gap, Dr. Hardesty." She extended her hand.

He took it. Her hand was small, but firm and capable in his.

"Call me Grant. After all, we're going to be working closely for the next month."

"Fine." The reservation was still there in her dark brown eyes. "Grant."

He'd held her hand a little longer than necessary. He released it and glanced around, looking for some topic that would ease the tension between them.

"This is a lot nicer than the temporary doc's quarters."

The big square kitchen had exposed beams in the corners and crossing the ceiling, with rough white plaster between them. Old-fashioned dish cabinets with multipaned glass fronts lined one of the walls, and a wood-burning stove took up floor space on the worn linoleum. In the corner nearest the door, she had a square oak table, its surface worn with the scars of countless meals.

Maggie managed a more genuine smile. "You should have seen it when I moved in."

"I can imagine." He saw the work she must have put in, now that he looked for it. The faded linoleum was spotless and brightened by rag rugs in bright colors. Someone, presumably Maggie, had polished the wood-burner to a black gloss. Red-and-white-checked curtains dressed the three small windows, and each windowsill sported a red geranium.

"No one had lived here for a lot of years. I had to fight the mice for control of the kitchen." Satisfaction laced her words, and she glanced around possessively.

"I suppose the cat helped."

"Callie?" Her face softened as she glanced at the white-orange-and-black ball of fur. "Callie's way too old for much mouse-catching, but we get along okay."

"How long have you been here?" He leaned his hip against the counter, wondering if she'd ask him to sit. Or if she was just waiting for him to leave.

"Five years."

Something shadowed her face when she said that— some emotion he couldn't quite decipher.

"You've made a nice nest here." He sniffed the aroma filling the kitchen—apples and cinnamon, he thought. "Is that the pie I smell?"

She nodded. "Aunt Elly always claims I'm her one failure in teaching the fine art of crust-making."

"If that means she bakes for you, failure might be worthwhile."

"Don't you dare tell her that."

Her smile was the first genuine one he'd seen directed at him. It lit the face he'd been thinking plain, brightening her cheeks and making her eyes sparkle. He realized he was leaning toward her without meaning to.

"I promise," he said solemnly.

"Well." She glanced toward the pot on the stove, her color still heightened. "Supper's almost ready. Aunt Elly left us stew and biscuits. Why don't you stay and eat with us? I know you can't have gotten any food in yet."

He hadn't even thought that far. "Thanks, but I can just go out and grab a bite."

"Not unless you want to make do with a sandwich from the general store. The café doesn't serve supper except on weekends."

He really was in the boonies. "In that case, I'll set the table."

"You don't have to do that." She lifted a stack of plates and bowls from the cabinet.

He took them from her hands. "My pleasure."

It only took minutes to set the scarred table. Maggie poured milk from a mottled enamel pitcher and scooped stew into bowls, then called the children.

Joey gave him a sidelong look as Grant slid onto a chair. "He staying for supper?"

"Yes." Maggie's return gaze was cautionary. "You be polite, you hear?"

"We'll get along fine, as long as Joey doesn't try to repair my furnace again." Grant studied what he could see of the kid's averted face. "What made you decide to work on the furnace, anyway?"

Thin shoulders shrugged. "I dunno."

He wanted to pursue it, but Maggie held out her hand to him. Startled, he took it, then realized they were all holding hands around the table. Joey frowned at him, ducking his chin. Apparently they were going to pray.

"Father, we ask You to bless this food." Maggie's warm, intimate tone suggested she spoke to a friend. "Please bless and protect Nella and bring her back to us soon." There was an almost imperceptible pause. "And we ask Your blessings on the guest at our table, Lord. Make his time here fruitful. Amen."

He didn't remember the last time anyone had prayed for him. It made him uncomfortable and touched him simultaneously. He and God hadn't been on speaking terms in years, but he didn't suppose he'd ever tell Maggie that.

"Good stew." Joey was well into his bowl already.

Maggie caught Grant's eyes and smiled. "He's a growing boy. He eats like a bear."

Joey growled, making his little sister and brother laugh. The kid's answering grin was pleased.

The girl, Tacey, was a mouse of a child, thin and shy, with light brown hair tumbling into her eyes in spite of the pink plastic barrette that was pinned in it. The smaller boy laughed at Joey's antics, then glanced around as if maybe he shouldn't have.

An interesting combination. Maggie seemed to lose that perennial chip on her shoulder when she talked with the kids. Her brown eyes warmed with caring.

When he'd first seen her that afternoon, he'd thought he was looking at an overworked nurse with an antipathy toward outsiders, doctors or both. Now he saw another side to Maggie, one that was ruled by protectiveness toward the three kids, the old cat and probably also the elderly woman.

She glanced up and caught him watching her. Her eyes widened, and for an instant he didn't hear the children's chatter. Their gazes caught and held. Awareness stretched between them like a taut cord.

Maggie broke the contact first, looking down at her bowl, her cheeks pinker than they'd been before. He yanked his attention to his stew, stirring the brown gravy as if that was the only thing on his mind.

What had just happened?

No sense asking the question. He already knew the answer. He'd looked at Maggie and felt a shockingly strong wave of attraction. Maggie had felt it, too.

That wouldn't do. He rejected the temptation. This month would be difficult enough without that kind of entanglement.

A pleasant, professional relationship—that was what was called for here. Maybe he shouldn't have tried to move beyond that instant antagonism. Maybe he should have settled for being sparring partners with Maggie, because anything else was out of the question.

Maggie stood at the reception desk checking charts. At least, she should have been checking charts. She definitely should not be thinking about those moments at supper last night when attraction had sparked between her and Grant.

She couldn't dismiss the memory. Like the proverbial elephant in the living room, it took up too much space.

She couldn't ignore the warm wave that had washed over her, waking every cell in her body and reminding her she was alive.

*All right, be rational.* She couldn't pretend that moment hadn't happened, but she could understand her reactions. After all, she hadn't had anyone special in her life for a long time—since she'd come back to Button Gap, in fact. She could hardly be surprised if working in close quarters with an attractive man roused feelings that were better left sleeping.

Grant *was* attractive. With his classically handsome face and his assured manner, he looked like what she suspected he was—a sophisticated, upper-class urbanite who'd been born with a silver spoon in his mouth. A greater contrast to herself couldn't be imagined.

Well, she wasn't trying to measure his suitability for her, was she? She'd simply recognized the feeling for what it was and shut it down. She'd shut down worse emotions than this in her life. She could handle it.

She shuffled the charts into a stack and plopped them firmly on the desktop. No problem.

The exam room door opened. Grant came out with a patient—old Isaiah Martin, come to see if the new doctor could do anything about his "rheumatiz."

"Just see if those new pills help you." Grant carried a parcel wrapped in brown paper gingerly in one hand. "Check in with us next week."

"Thanks, Doc." Isaiah tucked a handful of pill samples into the pocket of his dusty corduroy jacket, waved to Maggie and limped out, banging the door behind him.

Grant turned to her with a grin and held out the package. "What am I supposed to do with this?"

A parade of butterflies fluttered through her stomach at the grin. Okay, maybe she hadn't eliminated the feelings. She could still settle for controlling her reactions so Grant never suspected.

She took the parcel and peeked inside. "Well, I'd suggest refrigerating it until you're ready to eat it." At his blank look, she smiled. "It's venison sausage. Haven't you ever had any?"

"Not that I can recall. I take it the barter system is alive and well in Button Gap." He leaned against the desk, way too close for her state of mind. "Don't they realize that the county pays the bills?"

She carried the package to the small refrigerator. "People here don't like to accept charity. I've tried explaining that their tax dollars support the clinic, but most folks still want to pay their way."

He shook his head. "They're out of step with society, then."

"That's not a bad thing."

"No." His smile warmed those cool blue eyes. "Anyway, you can have the sausage if you want it."

"What's the matter? Too rough for your sophisticated palate?"

Instead of responding with a smile or a jibe, he studied her face for a moment, as if wondering what lay beneath the skin. "That sounds like a criticism," he said. "And I'm not sure why. What do you have against me, Maggie?"

She shouldn't have let the remark pop out of her mouth. She knew better.

Grant waited, expecting an answer. At least he didn't look angry.

"Sorry." She forced herself to be honest with him. "I guess the problem is that I see the volunteers come and go. Don't get me wrong. I'm grateful. We couldn't run the clinic without them."

"I sense a 'but' coming." He folded his arms across the front of the white lab coat he wore over a pale blue dress shirt.

She shrugged. "But sometimes they're more trouble than they're worth. And sometimes I get the feeling that the only reason they're here is to fill in the line for public service on their résumés."

"That's a pretty harsh judgment, isn't it?"

That was what Aunt Elly had said, in different words. She'd reminded Maggie that being judgmental was a sin.

"That's how I feel. If I'm wrong, I'm sorry."

He shoved himself away from the desk and came toward her, frowning. She had to force herself not to back up. He stopped, inches from her, his gaze intent on her face.

"Okay, fair enough. Why are you here, Maggie?"

*Not for any reason I'd like to confide in you.* "That's a long story."

"Give me the condensed version." He didn't look as if he intended to move until she did.

She looked up at him, then was sorry. He was too close for her state of mind. The tiny refrigerator was at her back, and he filled the narrow confines between the desk and the wall. She couldn't walk away without brushing against him, and she wouldn't do that. She had to say something.

"I worked in Pittsburgh for a time after I finished school, but I never got rid of my longing for the mountains. Button Gap felt like home to me, and I heard the county needed someone to run the clinic. So I came. End of story."

"It's a nice story." His voice had lowered to a baritone rumble that did funny things to her. His fingers brushed hers. "You're a dedicated person, Maggie."

Her breath caught in her throat. Warmth seemed to emanate from his touch, flowing through her. She wanted to lean into him and feel that warmth encircle her.

She couldn't.

What she'd told him wasn't the whole story, and a large part of her particular story wasn't nice at all.

That was just one more reason why she shouldn't be letting herself feel anything at all when Grant was around. Unfortunately, that seemed easier said than done, especially when he looked at her with what might be admiration in his eyes.

"Grant, I—"

The door sounded, flooding her with relief. He moved, and she slipped around him. Aunt Elly came toward them. The heavy wool jacket she wore had probably belonged to her late husband, and she carried a basket over her arm, with a napkin tucked over something that smelled of cinnamon.

"Those aren't cinnamon buns, are they?" Maggie leaned against the counter, smiling in welcome.

Movement beyond the plate-glass window caught her eye, and the smile faded. A county sheriff's car pulled into the parking space in front of the clinic.

She felt instantly guilty, and it didn't do any good to tell herself that the presence of the sheriff's car meant nothing. It might well mean trouble if Grant was here when the occupant of that car came inside.

She rounded the counter quickly, taking Aunt Elly's arm.

"You're just in time to see the doctor." She glanced meaningfully at the car, then back at Aunt Elly's face. "Keep him busy," she mouthed.

Aunt Elly followed her gaze, startled, then nodded. Her eyes sparkled with mischief. "That's good. I want to talk to the doc about my knee."

"You go on back." She yanked open the file drawer to pull out Aunt Elly's chart and hand it to Grant. "Dr. Hardesty's coming right now."

Only Grant's slightly lifted eyebrows indicated he thought she was rushing them. He took Aunt Elly's arm, and together they disappeared into the exam room.

Just in time. As the exam room door closed, the front door opened. Deputy Sheriff Gus Foster ambled toward the desk.

At least the sheriff's department had sent someone she knew. *Thank You, Lord.*

"Hey, there, Maggie, how's life treating you?" Gus lifted the dark felt hat from his white hair. With his snowy hair and beard and his comfortably round stomach, Gus visited the Button Gap schoolchildren as Santa every year.

"Fine, Gus. And yourself?" The formalities had to be gotten through before Gus would get to the reason for his visit, but her stomach tightened with the fear that Grant would come back out for some reason.

"Can't complain." He leaned against the desk. "Hear you've got a new doc."

She nodded. "From Baltimore. Just until Christmas." Had they'd chatted enough? It felt like her nerves were rubbed raw. "What brings you in to see us?"

"Well, now." A shade of reluctance, maybe even embarrassment, touched Gus's ruddy face. "It's this way. We had a call from Mrs. Hadley."

Maggie's stomach lurched. Mrs. Hadley, head of the county's social services department, wouldn't have called the sheriff's office for fun. Her thoughts flickered to the Bascom kids, safely tucked away with retired teacher Emily Davison for the afternoon, except for Joey, who was in school.

"What does she want now?" She tried to keep both face and voice expressionless.

"Now, Maggie, I know the two of you don't get along. Reckon I know why, too. But I can't ignore her when

she calls." He gave a wry grin. "Leastways, not unless
I want her trampling over my head again."

"If you know how she is—"

"I've got a job to do," he said with heavy finality.
"Mrs. Hadley's had her eye on Nella Bascom and her
kids. She stopped by to see them a couple of times and
didn't find anybody home. She wants to know what's
going on."

Her heart sank. She'd been hoping against hope that
the woman had enough to do without running all the
way up to Button Gap. She'd prayed that no official
notice would be taken of Nella's absence before she was
back home with her kids.

"Why did you come to me?" She tried to sound
unconcerned.

Gus didn't look convinced. "Everybody knows you've
been helping Nella get by since that no-count husband
of hers sent himself to perdition by crashing the logging
truck. I figured you might know something."

She could tell him Nella had gone away for a few
days, leaving the kids with her, but that would only lead
to more questions. "I don't." Another lie.

*I'm sorry, Lord. I don't want to lie, but what choice
do I have? Mrs. Hadley would snatch those kids away
in a minute. Nobody knows that better than I do.*

"What business is it of Mrs. Hadley's what the
Bascoms do, anyway?"

"Now, Maggie. The way I see it, if something comes
to my notice, official-like, I'd have to do something
about it. If not, well, I don't."

Her tension eased. "Thanks, Gus."

"I'm not saying I know anything. But you want to be careful."

The exam room door opened, and a wave of panic raced through her. "I'll be careful." She rounded the desk, wanting to hurry Gus out.

He straightened, immovable. "You know as well as I do that those paper-pushers at the county seat would just as soon close down the free clinic if somebody gave them a reason."

"Close down?" Grant stalked into the outer office, frowning. "What's going on? Can I help you, Officer?"

Maggie looked at Aunt Elly, who gave a helpless gesture seeming to indicate that she'd done everything she could to hold him back.

"Nothing's going on," she said. "Dr. Hardesty, this is Deputy Sheriff Foster. Gus is an old Button Gap boy, just stopping in to say hi."

Gus extended his hand. "Welcome to Button Gap, Doc. Hope you enjoy your stay here."

"I'll enjoy it more if I don't hear talk about closing down the clinic," Grant said, shaking hands. "What did you mean?"

Maggie held her breath.

"Oh, that's nothing." Gus smacked his hat against the side of his leg. "Maggie's an old friend. I was just teasing her."

*Thank you.* She should have known Gus wouldn't give her away to an outsider.

Aunt Elly bustled between them. "Gus, I'll give you a

cinnamon bun for a ride in that sheriff's car." She swung the basket in front of him.

Gus patted his stomach. "Always room for one of your cinnamon buns, but I don't want to deprive the doc."

"Plenty for everyone." Aunt Elly handed Gus a napkin-wrapped bun from the basket. She took his arm. "Now let's see about that ride."

"You've got it." Smiling, he escorted her to the door. "Nice to meet you, Doc. Be good, Maggie."

The door closed behind them. Maggie drew in a relieved breath.

Grant grasped her arm to turn her toward him. One look at his frown told her that her relief had been premature.

"What was that all about?"

She tried for a casualness she didn't feel. "Nothing. You heard Gus. He just likes to tease me."

"About closing down the clinic?"

She shrugged. "He has an odd sense of humor."

"It didn't sound like teasing to me." His mouth was set in an uncompromising line. His determined gaze pinned her to the spot, demanding answers she wouldn't give.

"Look." She pulled her arm free, letting annoyance show in her face. "I can't help what you thought it sounded like. Gus and I both know that some of the penny-pinchers in county government would be happy to close down the clinic, so they could do something else

with our tax dollars. But that's not going to happen."
*Please, God.*

"I'm glad you feel so confident about it." His eyes
were the blue-gray of a stormy sky.

"I do."

He wasn't satisfied—she could see that. But there
wasn't anything he could do. As long as he didn't learn
the truth about the Bascom children, they were safe.

"I hope you're right, Maggie. Because I have no
intention of letting the clinic be shut down while I'm
in charge here."

He tossed Aunt Elly's chart onto the desk and stalked
back toward the office. The door banged behind him.

*Lord, what else could I do? I have to protect those
kids.*

She had to. But there was one thing she *didn't* have
to do any longer.

She didn't have to worry about any more moments
when attraction sparked between her and Grant. He'd
obviously decided she wasn't to be trusted.

## Chapter Three

Grant prodded the limp green beans in the frozen dinner he'd just taken from the elderly oven. Saturday night, and he was dining on what looked like leftovers from the hospital cafeteria. If he were back in Baltimore, he'd probably be eating seafood at Thompson's with friends or a date.

He glanced at the clock. Well, no. He wouldn't have dinner anywhere near this early on a Saturday night in his normal life. Here in Button Gap, without city lights to dispel it, the November darkness seemed darker, the hour later.

Picking up his plate, he wandered into the living room and settled into the faux leather recliner in front of the television. This wasn't exactly the right ambience for dining, but it beat sitting at the Formica table in the kitchen.

He'd been in the village for nearly a week, and he had to confess the time had gone quickly. After a couple of quiet days, things had picked up at the clinic. Routine cases, for the most part, but they had kept him busy enough to forget he was stuck in the middle of nowhere for the rest of the month.

*Okay, Hardesty, stop acting like a baby. Anyone would think this was a lifetime commitment.*

Three more weeks, and he'd be free to leave. So life in Button Gap wasn't exciting. So what? The benefits to his future career certainly outweighed a little discomfort and a hefty dose of boredom.

The clinic seemed to run effectively, in spite of the jolt he'd had at hearing some county bureaucrats wanted to shut it down. Maggie had been scrupulous in following clinic procedures. She'd even exchanged her jeans and flannel shirt for a lab coat worn over a sweater to ward off the drafts that slipped through the chinks in the frame building.

At least, he'd prefer to believe the chill in the air came from the drafts. Possibly, however, the frost might be emanating from Maggie.

Had he overreacted to that overheard conversation with the deputy sheriff? Judging from the coolness she'd shown him the past few days, Maggie certainly thought so.

He didn't have anything for which to apologize. He was the doctor, and any problems with the clinic would reflect badly on him. He could just imagine the reaction of Dr. Rawlins, the man he hoped would soon be his senior partner, to hearing that his pet project had closed down while Grant was in charge.

Still, Grant wouldn't mind seeing Maggie's smile again.

A knock was a welcome interruption. He swung the door open to reveal Aunt Elly, swathed in a plaid wool jacket several sizes too large, topped by a discordant plaid muffler.

"What brings you out on this cold night?" He ushered her inside and snapped off the television news.

"Cold? Wait 'til you've been through a winter here and then talk to me about cold." She loosened the muffler. "I came to bring you along to pageant tryouts."

The only thing that came to mind was Miss America. "Pageant tryouts?"

"The Christmas pageant," she said, as if it ought to be self-explanatory. "Everybody in Button Gap comes to church the night they pick the cast, just to cheer them on."

Apparently he couldn't escape the holiday, no matter where he went. "I'm afraid I don't have any dramatic talent."

"Shoot, you don't have to try out, boy. It's mostly kids anyway. But you ought to jump into Button Gap life whilst you're here. 'Sides, Maggie's directing it." She glanced at his discarded plate. "We have dessert after they pick all the parts, y'know. More kinds of homemade pies than you can count."

He didn't need any reminders of the Christmas season. On the other hand, he didn't want to hurt the old lady's feelings, and just about anything was better than sitting here staring at the television.

"Your company and homemade pies sounds like a winning combination." He reached for the jacket he'd hung on the bentwood coatrack next to the door. "You're on."

He pulled the door shut behind them and started to take Aunt Elly's arm to help her down the two steps to the street. She'd already trotted down herself.

"It looks like your knee is feeling better."

She glanced up as if startled, then nodded. "It comes and goes." She snuggled the muffler around her chin. "Smells like snow in the air."

They crossed the quiet street. No one else seemed to have ventured outside tonight, unless the hamlet's whole population was already at the church. He slipped his hand under Aunt Elly's elbow.

"You and Maggie are pretty close, aren't you?" The question came out almost before he realized he'd been thinking about Maggie.

"Everybody knows everybody in Button Gap, if they live here long enough."

"You wouldn't be evading the question, now, would you?"

He could almost feel her considering. She wouldn't answer anything she didn't want to—he felt sure of that.

She looked at him as if measuring his interest, and then seemed to make up her mind.

"Maggie lived with me for a bit, when she was eleven," she said. "Guess that made us close, no matter how many miles or years there might be between us."

He digested that. "But you're not really related."

"No." She shrugged. "Folks round here take care of each other when there's trouble, blood kin or not."

The white frame church was just ahead, its primitive stained-glass windows glowing with the light from within. A chord of music floated out on the chilly air, followed by a burst of laughter.

An urgency he didn't understand impelled him. "What kind of trouble?"

Aunt Elly stopped just short of the five steps that led up to the church's red double doors. He felt her gaze searching his face.

Then she shook her head. "I 'spect that's for Maggie to tell you, if she wants to."

She marched up the steps, and he had no choice but to follow.

The small church had a center aisle with pews on either side. At a guess, the sanctuary probably seated a hundred or so. Plain white walls, simple stained glass, a pulpit that had darkened with age but had probably never been beautiful—he couldn't imagine a greater contrast to the Gothic cathedral–style church of his boyhood.

The atmosphere was different, too. There, he recalled the hushed rustle of women's dresses, the soft whisper of voices beneath the swelling notes of the organ. Here, laughter and chatting seemed acceptable. More than half the people in the church were children, and they trotted around as comfortably as if they were on the playground.

"Okay, come on." Maggie, standing by the piano

at the front, had to clap her hands to make herself heard over the babble of voices. The deep red sweater she wore with her jeans brought out the pink in her cheeks.

"Let's have a look at everyone who wants to be a wise man," she announced. "Come up front, right…"

The end of that sentence trailed off when she saw him. Fortunately, the thunder of small feet would have drowned it out anyway.

Maggie's eyes narrowed as she looked from him to Aunt Elly. Irritation pricked him. She had no reason to look as if he didn't belong here. He'd been invited.

He'd have slid into the back pew, but Aunt Elly grasped his arm and marched him down the aisle to near the front. Their progress was marked by murmurs.

"There's the new doctor."

"Young, ain't he?"

"Hi, Doc."

He nodded to those who greeted him and tried to ignore the other comments. He slid into the pew after Aunt Elly with a sense of relief. Then he glanced toward the front and found Maggie still watching him.

She blinked as their gazes met and turned quickly toward the children, but not before he saw her color heighten.

"Well, that's great." She seemed to count the small figures who bounced in front of her. "I think we need to narrow this down a bit."

"Can't we have more than three kings?" one of the kids asked.

It was Joey, he realized. The boy's face shone with scrubbing and his blond hair had been plastered flat to his head.

So the little monster wanted to be one of the magi. Grant would have expected a shepherd or a donkey was more his speed.

"I don't think—" Maggie began.

Some mischievous part of his mind prompted him. "The Bible doesn't actually say there were three wise men," he pointed out. "Only that there were three gifts."

"That's right." The man in the pew in front of him turned, smiling, and extended his hand. "Welcome. You'd be Dr. Hardesty, of course. I'm Jim Michaels."

Pastor Michaels, to judge by the Princeton Theological Seminary sweatshirt he wore. Grant tensed as he shook hands, and had to remind himself to relax.

"Sorry, Reverend. I didn't mean to start a theological quarrel."

"Jim, please." The young minister had a wide smile, sandy hair and a faded pair of jeans to go with the sweatshirt, which looked new enough to suggest he hadn't been out of school long. "Discussion, not quarrel."

"I think we'll stick with the traditional three kings," Maggie said firmly.

She frowned at him, and he smiled back, unrepentant. This was different enough from the church he remembered that it didn't bring up unhappy memories. And he enjoyed watching take-charge Maggie being ruffled by a crew of rug rats.

"Three kings," she repeated, in response to a certain amount of sniveling. "But the rest of you get to be angels or shepherds. Won't that be fun?"

As she went on with the casting, he had to admit she seemed to have a talent for making people happy. Even the most reluctant angel was brought around by the promise of having a gold halo.

Pastor Jim kept up a quiet commentary about the pageant, which Maggie seemed to tolerate with an amused smile. Unlike the look she'd darted at him when he'd intervened, he noted.

Well, presumably Pastor Jim was her friend, along with everyone else in the sanctuary. He thought again about the bombshell Aunt Elly had dropped on their walk to the church. The trouble in Maggie's family must have been fairly serious for her to be farmed out to a neighbor at that age.

He studied Maggie's face as she announced the parts for the pageant. Did that uncertainty in her childhood account for her fierce protectiveness toward these people? Maybe so. He knew as well as anyone the influence a childhood trauma could have on the rest of a person's life.

"Let's finish up with a carol before we go downstairs for dessert." Maggie glanced toward Pastor Jim, who obediently seated himself behind the piano.

"What will it be?" he asked, playing a chord or two.

"'Away in a Manger,'" several children said at once.

"You've got it." He began to play.

Grant tried to open his mouth, to sing like everyone else.

*Away in a manger, no crib for his bed.*

But something had a stranglehold on his throat, and he seemed to see his brother's face, his eyes shining in the light of a thousand candles.

He'd thought he could cope with this, but the old anger and bitterness welled up in him so strongly that it was a wonder it wasn't written all over him.

Maggie had her arms around a couple of the children as they sang. She glanced at him, and apparently his expression caused her to stumble over a phrase.

Maybe his feelings *were* written on his face. All he could think was that the moment the song was over, he was out of there.

The expression on Grant's face when the children began to sing the old carol grabbed at Maggie's heart and wouldn't let go. Dr. Grant Hardesty, the man she'd thought had everything, looked suddenly bereft.

She couldn't have seen what she thought she'd seen. That glimpse into his soul shook her, rattling all her neat preconceptions about who and what he was.

The last notes of the carol still lingered on the air as people started to make their way to the church basement and the homemade pies. Grant looked as if he intended to head straight back the aisle and out the door.

Aunt Elly didn't give him the opportunity. She grabbed his arm as soon as they stood, steering him toward the stairs at the rear of the sanctuary.

Maggie followed, shepherding the flock of children

along the aisle. She was close enough to hear Aunt Elly as they reached the back of the church.

"Come along now." She hustled him toward the stairs. "You don't want to get last choice of the pie, do you?"

Grant was out of Maggie's sight for a few minutes as they started down. By the time she and her charges had reached the church basement, he had resumed his cool, well-bred expression. That brief moment when she'd glimpsed an inner pain might have been her imagination, but she couldn't quite make herself believe that.

The children scattered, some racing for the table, others searching for their parents. She hesitated. Should she go up to Grant and introduce him around? She hadn't brought him. That was clearly Aunt Elly's idea.

"Come on, Doc." Isaiah Martin, looking better dressed than he had been for his clinic visit, waved toward Grant. "Get up here and pick out a slab of pie."

Friendly hands shoved him toward the table on a wave of agreement. Feeding him was their way of welcoming him. Would he recognize that?

"Here you go, Doc." Evie Moore slid a piece of cherry pie onto a flowered plate. "That's my cherry pie, and you won't find better anywhere, if I do say so myself. Those cherries come right off my tree. Now, what else will you have?"

"That's plenty," he began. Then he stopped, apparently realizing from the offended expressions on the other women that he'd made a strategic mistake.

He wasn't her responsibility. Still, maybe she'd better rescue him. Maggie slipped closer.

"You'd better try all of them," she murmured. "You wouldn't want to insult anyone."

"I can't eat fourteen pieces of pie unless you want to let out my lab coats." He slanted a smile at her, apparently not surprised to find her at his elbow. "How about getting me out of this?"

Suppressing that little flutter his smile provoked, she took a knife and split the piece of pie, sliding part onto a different plate. "Let's give Dr. Hardesty a little sliver of each kind," she suggested.

The pie bakers greeted that with enthusiasm. Evie might be acknowledged as the best cherry pie baker, but no one else intended to be left in the dust. Before Grant escaped from the serving line, they'd managed to add slivers of dried apple, rhubarb, lemon meringue and mincemeat pie.

Maggie helped herself to coffee, then realized that Grant had headed straight for the table where Joey sat. Her nerves stood at attention.

By now, all five hundred and three residents of Button Gap knew about the warning Gus had delivered. They were all on the lookout for Mrs. Hadley. Everyone, in other words, but Grant.

She reached the table quickly. She thought Joey understood how important it was to keep quiet about their mother's absence, but kids were unpredictable, and it was her job to keep them safe.

Joey wore a rim of cherry around his mouth. "Sure is good pie," he said thickly.

"You better take it easy, or you won't be able to sleep

tonight." Relieved, Maggie slid into the seat next to Joey. Unfortunately, that put her directly across from Grant.

His level brows lifted. "Are you talking to Joey or to me?"

"Both of you."

"You're the one who made me accept all of this," he protested.

"You didn't want to insult anyone, did you?"

He glanced at the crowded plate. "If it's that or my arteries, I think I'll take the arteries." He took a bite of Evie's cherry pie, and then gave a sigh of pure pleasure. "Although this might be worth the risk."

Their smiles entangled, and her heart rate soared.

*You're mad at him, remember?* she reminded herself, but it didn't seem to be doing any good. Maybe she'd better concentrate on finishing her dessert and getting the kids home.

Unfortunately Grant seemed to be eating at the same rate she was. He put his plate on the dish cart right behind her, grabbed his coat while she was getting the kids into theirs and walked out the door when they did.

"It's chilly out here." He buttoned the top button of his jacket.

She nodded. "Winter comes early in the mountains. We usually have a white Christmas."

By Christmas, Nella would be safely home with her children, and one source of Maggie's concern would be taken care of. By Christmas, Grant would be back in his world, probably forgetting about Button Gap the moment he crossed the county line.

The kids romped ahead of them. Joey stopped in the middle of the deserted street. He spun in a circle, his arms spread wide. "Snow!" he shouted.

Maggie looked up. Sure enough, a few lazy flakes drifted down from the dark sky.

"It is snow." She felt the featherlight touch of a snowflake on her cheek. "Look!"

Her foot hit a pothole in the road, and she stumbled. Grant's arm went around her in an instant, keeping her from falling.

"You're as bad as the kids." His voice was low and teasing in her ear. "Next thing you know you'll be dancing in the street."

"Is that so bad?"

She looked up at him and knew immediately she'd made a mistake. Grant's face was very close, his eyes warm with laughter instead of cool and judging. His arm felt strong and sure, supporting her.

The laughter in his eyes stilled, replaced by something questioning, even longing. Nothing moved—no one spoke. The children's voices were a long way off, and the world seemed to move in a lazy circle.

He was going to kiss her. She couldn't let that happen. She had to stop it.

But she couldn't. Whatever her reasonable, responsible brain said, her body had an entirely different agenda.

It didn't happen. Grant seemed to wake himself, as if from a dream.

"Well, maybe we'd better say good-night." There was something almost questioning in the words.

"Yes." She could only hope she didn't sound as stupid as she felt. "Good night."

She turned and ran after the children, knowing she was trying to run from herself.

Grant let out a sigh of relief as Maggie closed the outer door of the clinic behind the final patient on Monday afternoon and snapped the lock. She flipped the sign to Closed, not that it would actually stop anyone.

"Are we really done for the day?"

He'd been busier than this in the hospital emergency room, of course. Certainly he'd worked longer hours, especially as an intern. But somehow the clinic seemed a heavier responsibility, maybe because there was no one here to back him up except Maggie.

"That's the last of them." Maggie gathered files from the desk. "Congratulations."

He lifted an eyebrow, trying not to think about how soft her lips looked, or how he'd almost made the mistake of kissing them on Saturday night. "For what?"

"That was a good catch on Elsie Warner's pregnancy. Some docs wouldn't have seen it."

He shrugged. "Hopefully it will be nothing, but the ultrasound will tell us for sure. Better to be forewarned than caught unprepared."

It had been routine, of course. There was no reason to feel elated at the glow of approval in Maggie's eyes.

"Well, you did a good job. And you've been accepted.

That steady stream of patients means that the word has gotten around that you're okay."

He considered that, ridiculously pleased. "Sure it wasn't just the lure of a free checkup?"

"I told you, they don't take charity." She nodded toward the desk's surface. "You now have three jars of preserves, two of honey, a pound of bacon from the hog the Travis family just slaughtered and a couple of loaves of homemade bread."

He took a step nearer to Maggie, reminding himself not to get too close. He didn't want to feel that irrational pull of attraction again, did he?

"So deluging me with food is the sign of acceptance in Button Gap?"

"It is." Her full lips curved in a smile. "Don't tell me the big-city doc actually appreciates that."

"Hey, nobody ever brought me honey before." He picked up a jar, holding it to the light to admire the amber color. "You sure this is safe?"

"Of course it's safe." Her exasperated tone seemed to set a safety zone between them. "Toby Watkins's bees produce the best honey in the county."

"Well, I can't eat all this stuff on my own, and you have kids to feed. We'll share."

"You could take some back home to Baltimore with you when you go. Give it to your family."

He shook his head. "My mother doesn't eat anything but salads and grilled fish, as far as I can tell." He grimaced. "She might gain an ounce."

He tried to picture his cool, elegant mother in Button Gap. Impossible.

"You live with your family, do you?"

"No." He clipped off the word. The Hardesty mansion, as cool and elegant as his mother, hadn't been a place anyone could call home in years. But he wouldn't tell Maggie that.

"I have an apartment close to the hospital. It only made sense to be nearby when I was doing my internship and residency."

"Will you stay there when your month here is up?"

"Well, that depends." He put the jar down, and his hand brushed hers. At once that awareness he'd been avoiding came flooding back.

And they were alone in the quiet room with dusk beginning to darken the windows.

Maggie cleared her throat, as if she'd been visited by the same thought. "Depends on what?"

"In a way, on what happens here." He folded his arms across his chest, propped his hip against the table and kept talking to block feeling anything. "I'm being considered for a place in one of the best general practices in the city. The chief partner is a big supporter of the Volunteer Doctors program."

Maggie stared at him. "Is that why you came here? To impress him?"

"He suggested it. He said volunteering would be good experience—that I'd learn to relate to patients in a whole new way."

Actually, Dr. Rawlins had been rather more direct than that.

*Technically, you're a good doctor, Hardesty, but you keep too thick a wall between yourself and your patients. I don't want a physician who gets too emotional, but I have to see some passion. Maybe you'll find that if you get into a new situation.*

Rawlins was the best, and Grant wanted that partnership. So he'd taken the advice, even though he wasn't sure passion was his forte. Being a good physician ought to be enough.

"And is it working?" Maggie's question was tart, and he remembered what she'd said about volunteers coming here to pad up their résumés.

Anger welled up, surprisingly strong. She didn't have the right to judge him.

"What's wrong, Maggie? Isn't that an altruistic enough motive for you?"

She stiffened, hands pressed against the desk. "It's none of my business why you came."

"No? Then why are you looking at me as if you're judging me?"

"I'm not." She turned away, the stiffness of her shoulders denying the words. "I suppose we're just lucky that our needs happen to coincide with yours."

They were lucky. The people of Button Gap got his services for a month at no cost to the community, and he got the experience he needed to land the position he wanted. It was a fair exchange.

So it didn't matter to him in the least that knowing his motives had disillusioned Maggie.

Not in the least.

## Chapter Four

"You sure keeping the boy out of school is the only way of handling this?" Aunt Elly still looked worried on Tuesday morning as Maggie headed for the office.

Maggie paused, wishing she didn't have to hide Joey away from his friends. Was she overreacting? Letting her own fear of the county social worker govern what she did with the children? The memory of the deputy's visit was too fresh in her mind to allow her to judge.

"I know he doesn't want to stay home."

She glanced toward the living room, where Joey was trying to convince his siblings to play school. They didn't seem impressed with the idea of sitting still.

"I just don't know what else to do. If he's in school, it's too easy for Mrs. Hadley to find him."

Aunt Elly gave her a searching glance, as if plumbing the depths of Maggie's soul. "What did his teacher have to say about it?"

"She agreed it was just as well." Nobody at the small Button Gap elementary school would want to give them away, but they also couldn't risk running afoul of the county. "That way they're not to blame. It's not long until Christmas vacation anyway, and Emily Davison will tutor him. He won't fall behind."

"Guess maybe it's for the best." Aunt Elly's agreement sounded reluctant, but really, what else could they do? "How are you going to explain it to Grant?"

Her fingers clenched. "I'm not." She shook her head. "Honest, we can't take the chance. He can't know about Joey being out of school."

"I don't want to lie to the man." Aunt Elly's blue eyes darkened. "I'm not saying I won't, in a good cause, but I surely don't want to."

"We can't risk telling him the truth." Aunt Elly might think Grant could be trusted, but Maggie wasn't so sure. She kissed the older woman's cheek, its wrinkles a road map of the life of service Aunt Elly had lived. "Trust me. We can't depend on him."

Aunt Elly nodded, clearly still troubled. "I'll go along with you, child. But keep your mind open. The doc might be a better man than you take him for."

Maggie slipped out the door, shrugging her jacket closer for the short walk to the clinic's door. Aunt Elly always gave everyone the benefit of the doubt.

*We can't depend on him.* She didn't even *want* to depend on the man. He was an outsider, and he didn't mean a thing to her except as an obstacle to keeping those children safe. Not a thing.

She opened the clinic door. Grant, in the hallway pulling on a lab coat, turned to her with a smile lighting his normally serious face. Her heart gave a rebellious jump.

"Morning."

She concentrated on hanging up her jacket. What did Grant have to smile at, anyway? Certainly the last words that had passed between them the day before had been anything but friendly. She reached for her lab coat, only to find that Grant was already holding it for her.

"Thank you."

"Sure." His hands brushed her shoulders as she slipped the coat on.

With an effort, she steadied her breath and took a step away from him. It was just the effect of his closeness in the dim, narrow hallway—that was all. She certainly didn't have any longing to lean against him or to rely on him. Absolutely not.

"You came in early." She slipped past him, rounding the corner into the reception area and snapping on the overhead light.

He followed, leaning against the door frame. The harsh light picked out the fine lines around his eyes, the slant of his cheekbone. His usual neat pants, pale blue dress shirt and lab coat seemed to advertise the fact that he was out of his sphere.

"There's not much else to do. What's on our plate for today?"

Grant sounded determined to be friendly if it killed him. He'd probably decided that it didn't pay for the two of them to be at odds.

She might feel that way, too, if she weren't weighed

down with the secret she had to keep, to say nothing of that ridiculous little flutter she felt every time he got too close.

She sat down at the desk and glanced over the list of appointments. "This looks pretty routine, but I imagine we'll have some walk-ins. Cold and flu season is on us already."

"Nothing like having a waiting room full of people sharing their germs." He leaned over her shoulder to look at the schedule, running his finger down along the list.

His nearness made her voice tart in self-defense. "People come because they're sick, remember?"

His hand paused on the schedule, then pressed flat. "Come on, Maggie, give me a break. You know I was kidding."

"Sorry."

That abrupt word certainly didn't sound very gracious. Aunt Elly would be ashamed of her, if she heard. She took a breath, trying to find something better to say. The trouble was, she just couldn't forget why he was here.

Grant leaned against the desk and folded his arms across his chest, looking down at her. He did that disdainful expression really well. People like him were probably born with the ability.

"What is it, Maggie? Are you still bothered by my motives for volunteering?"

She pushed her chair back, its wheels squeaking, to put another few inches between them. "I'm sorry," she said again, knowing she still didn't sound convincing. "It's really none of my business why you're here."

"That's right—it's not." His lips tightened. "Most people have a little self-interest in what they do. Probably even you, truth be told."

"I don't know what you mean. I'm here because they need me here."

"And because you like to be needed." He whipped the words back at her.

For a moment, all she could do was stare at him. "That's not true." Was it? She tried to search her conscience, but that wasn't easy when she was feeling thoroughly annoyed with him.

He shrugged, as if it didn't really matter to him at all. "Have it your way. The point is that your motives don't affect the care you give people. Nor do mine."

They'd drifted into dangerous territory. She had no desire to let Grant Hardesty know anything about the forces that drove her. That was between her and God.

She took a steadying breath. *I need to get out of this conversation, Lord. I can't afford to say one more thing that annoys him.*

"You're right." She stood, because she couldn't sit there any longer with him looking down at her. "I don't have any complaint about the care you're giving our patients. We're lucky to have you, no matter why you came."

She started to brush past him, but he didn't move. She cleared her throat.

"I'd better get the door unlocked. It's almost time to open."

He looked at her for another moment, then stepped back to let her go by. As she did, she glanced at his face and then was sorry.

She'd created a barrier between them with her attitude. She shouldn't have done that. The last thing she needed was to make Grant any more annoyed and suspicious than he already was.

"Take a deep breath for me."

Grant listened to the patient's breathing sounds, realizing he'd been functioning on automatic pilot for the past half hour. That was Maggie's fault, actually. He was still conducting a silent argument with her in his head.

Why couldn't he just dismiss her opinions for what they were?—the typical self-righteous proclamations of a woman who thought people had to have the highest of motives for every single thing they did.

Probably because he didn't really believe that. Maggie might be prickly, but she did have the best interests of Button Gap at heart.

She belonged here. He didn't. It was as simple as that. For a moment he seemed to see her the way she'd been Saturday night at the church, her eyes lit with laughter as she joked with the children, her face glowing.

Not a helpful image. He was not attracted to Nurse Maggie, not in the least.

He took the stethoscope from his ears and made eye

contact with the elderly woman who'd fulfilled Maggie's prediction about cold and flu season starting.

"That doesn't sound too bad. You go ahead and get dressed, and I'll leave a prescription at the desk with Maggie. Take the pills and get some rest, and you'll be feeling better in no time."

Her thanks followed him as he strode out of the exam room door.

He was trying to take this morning at his hospital pace, he realized. He may as well slow down. There was no point in rushing through the Button Gap clinic as if it were a city hospital—he couldn't even see the next patient until the current one was out of the exam room.

Inefficient. He frowned. Maybe he ought to give Dr. Rawlins some suggestions about running the clinic more efficiently.

He rounded the corner, to see Maggie leaning across the counter in animated conversation with someone in the waiting room. Any suggestions he made wouldn't reflect adversely on Maggie. He was thinking about the physical setup, not the staff.

He tossed the file on the scarred oak desk as she turned toward him. He pulled the prescription pad from his pocket. "I'm giving Mrs.—what was her name?"

"Robbins. Addie Robbins."

He scribbled quickly. No use trying to slow down. Ingrained habits died hard. "I'm giving her an antibiotic for that bronchitis."

He ripped off the script and handed it to her. She

looked at it, frowning. He could almost hear her thinking.

"What?" he snapped. She had some criticism loitering in her mind, he could sense it.

"Maybe it would be better if you considered prescribing—"

He slapped his palm down on the desk. Then, mindful of the room full of waiting patients, he jerked his head toward the rear of the clinic.

"Come back to the office for a moment, Maggie. Please."

She pushed her chair back, and he heard her footsteps behind him as he stalked back down the hallway. As soon as they were inside the crammed office, he swung to face her.

"I'm the doctor, remember? I don't need you second-guessing me on the meds I prescribe. I don't need you second-guessing me on anything."

If his harsh words intimidated her, it didn't show. She just looked at him for a long moment, her dark eyes giving nothing away. Then she went to the glass-fronted cabinet against the wall and pulled out a box. She thrust it into his hands.

He looked at the contents of the box, frowning. "Drug samples. So what? If I say the patient should have a particular medicine—"

"A particular medicine that she'd have to drive twenty miles to get." Maggie's voice didn't betray any emotion, but her dark eyes narrowed dangerously. "If she had a car, which she doesn't. And even if she could get to the pharmacy, she couldn't afford the medication."

All of a sudden he was on shaky ground. He tried to regroup. "If she has to have it—"

Those soft lips of hers looked as if they were carved from ice. "If she has to have that particular antibiotic, I'll drive down and get it and pay for it myself. But if she doesn't have to have that particular one—" She jerked a sharp nod at the box in his hands.

"You want to give her the medicine."

"If we give her the antibiotic samples, saying the medicine is part of her office visit, she just might take the pills instead of going home and treating bronchitis with herbal tea and coneflower."

His irritation drained away. He looked again at the box's contents, packed tight with everything from beta blockers to Zithromax. "You've probably got enough to supply Button Gap for most of the winter. Where did you come by these?"

She shrugged. "Some of the drug reps know how hard up we are. They've been freehanded when it comes to samples." She glanced down briefly, then looked at him with a certain amount of caution. "I wasn't trying to second-guess you. I just wanted to be sure Addie got what she needed."

He lifted an eyebrow. "Don't you ever get tired of being right, Maggie?"

She looked startled, but then her face relaxed in a smile. "Careful, Doctor. I might remind you of that when you don't want to hear it."

That smile did nice things to her face. And he shouldn't be noticing that.

"Okay." He flipped quickly through the contents of the box and pulled out what he needed. "Give her these, and make sure she understands she has to take all of them. I don't want to see her back again because she decided to save some for a rainy day."

"Will do." She turned, then paused at the door. "Grant…thanks. I appreciate your listening to me."

"When you're right, you're right." It was easier to admit than he'd have expected. "Just don't make a habit of it."

Her eyes danced. "I'll try not to."

She was gone before he could say anything else. That was probably just as well.

He frowned absently at the dusty file cabinets. He and Maggie had moved from antagonism to an easy banter in a matter of moments. In most hospital circumstances that would be fine, but he and Maggie were alone here. They'd both be better off if they kept things strictly business.

But he had an uneasy suspicion that if he made Maggie laugh too often, "strictly business" would be a tough policy to follow.

She might actually begin to enjoy Grant's presence if she had a clear conscience. Maggie stacked patient files and glanced at the clock. Morning office hours were over—Grant would be out soon with the final patient. She'd lock the door, and then they'd be alone again.

And again, she'd be tempted to relax, to laugh with him, to talk. To tell him more than she should.

She touched the faint scar that crossed her collarbone. Faded now, it barely showed, but her fingers could trace the line. It was a vivid reminder of how easily a child could be hurt.

Of what her responsibilities were. She had to protect Joey and Tacey and Robby. There wasn't anyone else.

So she wouldn't let her guard down with Grant. She couldn't.

The exam room door opened, and Grant ushered the patient out. Maggie followed Evie Moore, who was still talking, to the doorway. She nodded, she smiled and once Evie was finally outside, she snapped the lock and flipped the sign to Closed.

"Will you look at this?" Grant put a cardboard box on the counter.

"I don't need to look—I can smell." The aroma drew her closer. "Evie brought you a whole cherry pie."

Grant flipped the lid back. Dark sweet cherries peeked through the flower-petal slits in the top crust.

"If this is anything like the one I had at the church the other night, I just might eat the whole thing myself."

"It's even better." Maggie inhaled, enjoying the rich scent, enjoying even more the relaxed look on Grant's face. "She got up early to bake this before she came. It's still warm from the oven."

He sniffed and sighed, the corners of his eyes crinkling. "Okay, Maggie, you and the kids have to help me with this. Otherwise I'll have an added fifteen pounds to show for my month in Button Gap."

"That's what you keep saying, but I don't see you turning anything down."

"Hey, nobody told me about the fringe benefits to volunteer doctoring. I might have come sooner if I'd known what awaited me."

His gaze was warm on her face, and for an instant it was almost as if he included her in the benefits he'd found in Button Gap. She pushed that thought away. It was silly. If he could have, Grant would probably have brought his own nurse with him on this assignment. Then he wouldn't have to argue all the time.

In an instant her imagination had created a picture of that perfect nurse—skilled, supportive, eager to serve.

She flicked the image away with the tip of an imaginary finger.

"So you think a few cherry pies and homemade preserves make up for the lack of coffee bars and fine restaurants?"

"Never been crazy about coffee bars." Grant took a plate and knife from the shelf next to the refrigerator and cut into the pie. Cherry juice shot out, making her mouth water. "Seafood restaurants—now them I miss. Baltimore has some of the best crab in the world."

"I know. I was there once. We ate down at the Inner Harbor."

"I hope you had steamed crabs." Grant handed her the pie and cut another slice for himself.

"I did, as a matter of fact." She smiled, remembering.

"It was the first time I'd ever seen a whole crab. I didn't know how to get into it."

He closed his eyes, as if remembering the tastes she'd conjured up, then shook his head. "It'll taste even better when I get back."

"Counting the days already?" she asked lightly.

"Not exactly." He shrugged, looking a bit surprised at himself. "Oddly enough, I'm not as impatient to be finished as I thought I would be. Maybe I'm actually learning something from this experience."

"Can I have that in writing? Maybe we can use your endorsement to recruit future volunteers."

Future volunteers. For an instant her smile faltered. Grant would leave, and someone else would come. That was the way things were.

He didn't seem to notice her momentary lapse. "Sure, I'll give the program an endorsement. How about—"

He stopped when the door at the back of the office opened. For an instant her heart seemed to stop, too, when Joey poked his head in.

"Maggie, can I have—" He sniffed. "Hey, you got pie in here?"

Grant waved his fork. "Come on in. You can help us eat this."

Maggie fought to control the tension that galloped along her nerves. What was Joey doing out of the house when she'd told him to stay put? And how long would it take Grant to realize the boy should be in school?

"He needs to have lunch first." She caught the boy's

shoulders and turned him toward the door. "You go on back to the kitchen. I'll bet Aunt Elly has lunch ready."

"But, Maggie—"

"Go on, now."

Grant slid a piece of pie onto a paper plate. "The woman's a slave driver, Joey. Here, have this after lunch."

Joey turned back to take the pie.

*Get him out of here,* her mind shouted. *Get him out fast, before Grant realizes he shouldn't be here.*

"Okay, off you go." She shepherded Joey and the pie to the door, then closed it behind him.

She could breathe again. Grant hadn't caught on.

She turned back to him, planting a smile on her lips. And found him looking at her with raised brows.

"Nice job, Maggie. You want to tell me why Joey isn't in school today?"

She'd relaxed too soon. And she didn't have a plausible story ready to offer him.

Grant folded his arms, waiting. "You're not going to tell me he's sick. The kid's the picture of health."

"No." She tried to force her limp brain to work. "I'm not going to tell you that."

"Well?" He shoved himself away from the desk, taking the two strides that covered the space between them. "What's the story, Maggie?"

This might have been easier if he'd stayed where he was. But he didn't want to make it easy, did he?

When she didn't speak, his gaze probed her face. "Something's wrong. What? You can tell me."

Could she? She wanted to. It would be such a relief to trust him.

But then Joey's face formed in her mind. For a moment it seemed her own face flashed before her, back when she'd been lost and alone.

No. She didn't know Grant well enough to trust him with a secret like this one. She never would.

She took a deep breath. "It's nothing that serious. Joey's just been…a little upset, that's all."

*Upset. That was putting it mildly. His world was turned upside down, but he was still managing to smile.*

"Upset about what?"

"About his mother being away." That part was true enough. The rest of the story held the difficulty.

"Natural enough. That doesn't explain why he isn't in school."

Grant certainly wouldn't make this easy.

"I talked with his teacher." Also true. "With his father's death only last month and his mother away, it's been hard on him."

She might as well stop rationalizing. The words were true enough, but all of the things she left out turned them into one big falsehood.

"We decided it might be better to keep him out of school for a few days. His mother will be back soon, and he'll settle down then. It's almost time for Christmas break anyway, and there's a retired teacher who's offered to give him some individual help."

She managed to look at Grant, gauging his reaction. He shook his head slowly.

"Poor little guy. I didn't realize he'd lost his dad so recently."

Joey was a poor little guy, but not for the reasons Grant supposed. "It's been a difficult time."

Grant touched her hand. "You're a good friend to help out this way." His eyes were as warm as his fingers against her skin. "If there's anything I can do, let me know."

"Thanks." She managed a smile. "I can't think of anything, but thanks."

Somehow it had been better when he'd doubted her and criticized her. His sympathy just made her feel worse. And if he ever learned the truth…

Well, she wouldn't need to worry about dealing with his sympathy then. He'd have none at all if he ever found out how she'd deceived him.

## Chapter Five

If guilt were a disease, she'd be flat on her back by now. Maggie beat the cookie batter with a wooden spoon, taking some pleasure in the vigorous activity, as if the batter were to blame for her predicament.

Unfortunately, she was the only one at fault, and she knew that perfectly well. For the past two days she'd been playing and replaying in her mind that conversation with Grant about the children, trying to find some better way of handling it.

She hadn't. She couldn't tell him the truth, and she couldn't stomach lying. So somehow, she'd have to learn to live with this uncomfortable feeling.

"Isn't it ready yet, Maggie?" Tacey propped her chin on the wooden table, her blue eyes huge in her small face.

"Almost ready." Maggie sprinkled flour on the table and then began rolling the cookie dough with the heavy wooden rolling pin Aunt Elly had given her. Maybe her piecrust always crumbled to pieces, but she had a good hand with Christmas cookies.

"I want to cut out a wreath." Tacey clutched a metal cookie cutter in one hand, tapping it against the table. "Can I?"

Maggie smiled at her, her heart filling. "You sure can, sweetheart."

At least she still knew one thing for sure, no matter how many sleepless nights it cost her. These children had to be protected until Nella came back.

"I don't want to do any old wreath." Joey scrambled onto a chair. "I'm gonna make a reindeer."

Robby reached up to snatch a piece of dough and pop it in his mouth, then looked around as if to be sure no one was watching.

"You can all make whatever you want," Maggie said. "They're your cookies. But remember, it's only right to share them."

Three little heads nodded solemnly. The Bascoms had never had much, but what they did have, they shared.

That was a sign of how good a mother Nella could be, now that Ted wasn't around to make her life a misery. As soon as Nella herself realized that—

*Soon, Lord. It will be soon, won't it? I know Nella needs to come back on her own, so she knows she's strong enough to do the right thing. But please, let it be soon.*

"Okay." Maggie made a final pass at the dough. "You guys can start cutting out, while I take the last batch out of the oven."

She moved to the stove, a blast of heat warming her face as she slid the cookie sheets out. She'd just put the trays on a cooling rack when someone knocked. Wiping her hands on a tea towel, she opened the door.

Grant stood on her doorstep, holding a sheaf of papers in his hand.

"Hi. Have you got a moment?" He glanced past her, obviously noting the children busy at the table. "It looks as if you haven't."

She didn't want to talk with him, not with the memory of her falsehoods making a heavy ball of guilt in her stomach. But she could hardly say so. She stepped back, holding the door wide.

"That's okay. Come in."

He stepped into the kitchen, sniffing appreciatively. "It always smells good in here."

"We're doing our Christmas cookie baking." She glanced at the kids, then realized Robby had just slid a whole section of dough onto the chair, covering himself with flour in the process.

"Hold on a sec." She rescued the dough, then dusted Robby off. "Let's keep everything on the table, okay?"

Robby nodded, stuffing another piece in his mouth.

She heard a low chuckle from behind her.

"I never knew cookie baking was so hazardous." Grant leaned over to look, keeping a careful distance between himself and the mist of flour in the air. "Maybe you ought to wear masks."

"A little flour never hurt anyone. You can't make cutout cookies without also making a mess."

She was suddenly aware of her appearance, her sweatshirt dotted with a fine white dust and her jeans probably bearing the marks where she'd wiped her hands. Grant, of course, looked spotless in khakis and a forest-green sweater.

"I wouldn't know about that," he said. "I've never made any cookies."

Immediately three pairs of blue eyes focused on Grant's face.

"You never made Christmas cookies?" Joey sounded incredulous. "Everybody makes Christmas cookies with their mama."

Was she imagining it, or did Grant's face stiffen?

"Not me," he said.

Tacey slid off her chair. She reached out tentatively and tugged at Grant's hand. "You can make my share," she whispered, as if afraid to speak out loud in his presence.

Maggie's throat tightened. Did Grant realize what a generous gift the little girl had offered?

No, of course he didn't. He didn't know that Tacey never voluntarily got within reach of a man's hand. He didn't know how rare something as simple as a quiet afternoon baking cookies was for her.

Grant looked down at the child with surprise and a hint of some other emotion flickering in his eyes. "I don't want to take yours," he said softly.

"We all share." Joey's voice was firm, and he gave Robby a look that dared him to disagree.

Robby nodded. "Share. Mommy says share."

Maggie waited for Grant to make some excuse that would take him right back out the door, but instead he nodded.

"Then I'd like to."

Well, so much for keeping Grant away from the kids. "If you're going to bake, you'd best take off that sweater. Or I have an apron you could wear."

The corner of Grant's mouth twitched. "Think I'll pass on the apron." He peeled off his sweater, revealing a cream button-down shirt. "Will this do?"

She nodded. "At least it's pretty much the same color as the flour. And you can wash it."

What was Grant doing about his laundry? It hadn't occurred to her to wonder. She suspected he wasn't used to doing it for himself.

"That's fine." He unbuttoned his cuffs and rolled the sleeves back. "I'm ready. Somebody show me what to do. Tacey?"

Afflicted with sudden shyness, Tacey shook her head, finger in her mouth.

"It's easy," Joey said. "Just press down with the cutter, like this, and then Maggie will help you put the cookie on the sheet."

"I imagine Dr. Grant can do that for himself," Maggie said.

Grant, head bent as he cut out a reindeer, tilted his face toward her. He smiled, a strand of brown hair falling onto his brow, his eyes crinkling. "I have to have Maggie's help, too. I'd probably break off a reindeer's leg if I tried to do it myself."

His smile had the same effect on her as opening the oven door had. She could only hope he'd think her rosy cheeks were from the baking.

"Maybe I'd better do it then." She cut out a church-shaped cookie. "We wouldn't want the doctor to cause a trauma."

His lips quirked. "You might have to report me to the county medical board."

"What's a tray-mom?" Joey's voice was loud, as if he'd noticed the byplay and didn't like it.

"Trauma," she corrected. "It's an injury."

The boy frowned. "Like when I got my arm broke?"

Her stomach cramped. "Like that," she agreed. None of the Bascoms had ever budged from their story that Joey had broken his arm falling out of the apple tree last spring. She'd had her own ideas about how he'd been hurt, but no proof.

"All ready, Nurse." Grant straightened. "Will you transfer the patient to the cookie sheet?"

Joey grinned as she slid the spatula carefully under the reindeer. "Betcha can't do it, Maggie."

"You're saying that because you know reindeer are the hardest. Just a little more—"

The reindeer's foreleg crumbled.

"Broken," Tacey whispered.

Grant chuckled. "Looks as if we'll have to set the patient's leg."

He reached across the table, his arm brushing Maggie's as he molded the dough back together again. Another wave of warmth swept over her. Really, if the man stayed around long enough, she wouldn't need much firewood for the winter.

"Done." Grant dusted off his hands. "I predict a full recovery."

Joey leaned over to inspect. "It'll break again when we take it off the pan," he predicted.

"The cookie will taste just as good," Maggie said. "Come on, now. Let's get this last tray finished, and soon it will be time to eat some."

Tacey was staring at Grant instead of cutting out her cookies. "Dr. Grant?" Her voice was as soft as a snowflake drifting to the earth. "Why didn't your mommy bake cookies with you?"

Grant was standing so close that Maggie could feel him stiffen at the question. Apprehension rose in her. If he snubbed the child for her innocent words…

He seemed to force a smile. "My mommy didn't like to do things like that."

"Didn't like to do things with you?" Clearly that was beyond Tacey's comprehension. "Why? Were you bad?"

She ought to intervene. Still, what could she say?

Grant's expression hadn't changed, but something lurked in the depths of his eyes that wrenched her heart. What kind of childhood had he had? She'd assumed that silver spoon he'd been born with protected him from hurt.

"No, I wasn't bad." His smile faltered for an instant. "Some people just don't like to do things with kids. You're lucky to have Maggie."

"And Mommy," Joey said quickly. "Mommy always makes cookies with us."

Robby's face clouded. "I want Mommy."

"She'll be back soon," Maggie said quickly, hoping to avert a storm. Robby, the youngest, cried the most over Nella's absence, though all three of them were affected. "Soon. You'll see."

If they weren't convinced, at least they didn't argue the point. They wanted to believe in Nella's return even more than Maggie did.

The children turned their attention back to the cookies. Maggie tried to watch Grant's face without him catching her doing it.

What had just happened? Her neat preconceptions about the kind of life Grant had led had taken a serious jolt. She actually felt a twinge of sympathy for the man she'd thought had everything.

She glanced again at his classic, composed features. Only a little tension around his mouth suggested that he'd been bothered by that exchange, or that he'd said more about himself than he'd intended to.

But he had. He'd shown her a piece of Dr. Grant Hardesty that he probably didn't often show to anyone.

Now how had that happened? Grant concentrated on pressing down the bell-shaped cookie cutter, because he didn't want to look at Maggie.

He didn't let other people know what he was feeling. Ever. All his friends got from him was what was on the surface.

If someone who'd known him since childhood was unwise enough to mention Jason, he ignored it. He had to. That was the only way he knew how to cope.

Carefully he shut thoughts of his brother back into the secret corner of his mind. Maggie didn't know about Jason, and she never would. As for that little piece of truth about his relationship with his mother—well, she could make of it anything she wanted.

Still, he hadn't expected to blurt that out. He could have deflected the child's question. Maybe Button Gap was having an effect on him. Dr. Rawlins would probably be pleased at that. He wasn't so sure that he was.

"Okay." Maggie transferred the last cookie sheet to the oven and dusted her hands on her jeans. Judging by the looks of those jeans, she'd been doing that all afternoon. "You guys go to the bathroom and wash up while I clean the table. Then you can have cookies."

That pronouncement resulted in a noisy stampede from the room. He could hear their feet thundering up the steps to the second floor.

"What about me?" He held out sticky hands. "Do I get sent upstairs, too?"

Maggie shook her head, smiling. "You can use the sink. I just wanted them out from underfoot while I clean up." She glanced at the kitchen floor. "Although cleaning up might take more time than I have."

He turned on the tap. "You have your hands full with those three, don't you?"

"I'm doing all right."

The thread of defensiveness in her voice made him turn to face her, hands under the stream of water.

"I wasn't criticizing, Maggie. You're a good person, to do so much for a friend."

She studied his face for a moment, as if measuring his meaning, then shrugged. "People around here take care of each other." She bent to scrub the sticky table surface, her shiny dark hair swinging down to hide her face. "That's just the way it is."

"I see that." He leaned against the sink, drying his hands. Wondering. "Aunt Elly told me you lived with her for a time when you were a child."

Her slim figure stilled. Was she surprised Aunt Elly had told him? Or was she just trying to think of a way of saying it was none of his business?

"That's right, I did." She swung to face him. "My family needed some help. Aunt Elly was there for us."

The words had a ring of finality about them. She clearly didn't intend to say more.

He was surprised at how much that annoyed him. Apparently she didn't feel that his small admission of family frailty warranted any similar confidence from her.

She slid the cooled cookies onto a platter and set it on the table, then got out a pitcher of milk. She hesitated, her gaze fixed on the cookie plate for a moment, then glanced at him as if trying to decide something. The children's feet thumped on the stairs.

"Aunt Elly took care of me," she said. "I'm taking

care of Nella's children. I guess I'm doing what she taught me by her kindness. I wish—"

The children came storming back into the room just then, and the fragile moment was gone. Whatever Maggie wished, he wouldn't hear it now, not with three hungry children converging on the table.

Joey grabbed for the cookie platter, his arm dangerously close to the milk pitcher. Robby bumped into him, the pitcher tipped, the milk sloshed and several cookies slid toward the floor.

"Joey!" Grant swung to catch the pitcher before it landed on the floor, too. "You've got to—"

The boy cowered away from him, arms up to shield his face. He stopped, stunned.

Something grabbed his heart and squeezed. Only one thing would make a child react like that. He could hardly breathe for the fury that choked him at the thought of someone harming that child.

He took a breath, forcing himself to be calm. He had to say something that would take that expression of fear off Joey's face.

Maggie beat him to it, catching the boy in a hug. "It's all right. Joey, it's all right, honest. No one will hurt you."

"I'm sorry." Joey's voice trembled on a sob. "I didn't mean to spill it."

"Hey, buddy, I know you didn't." Grant knelt next to him, making his voice soft. "I'm sorry I shouted. I wasn't mad at you. I just wanted to catch the milk before it spilled."

He could see the boy's rigidity ease. Maggie's eyes, wide and pained, met his over the child's head, and she nodded, as if telling him to keep talking.

"Listen, I'm not mad, really I'm not. I was startled, that's all."

Joey slowly unwound himself from Maggie's arms. It seemed to take an effort to look at Grant, but he managed. "Are you sure?"

"Positive." He suppressed the urge to ruffle the boy's hair. He'd better not make any more sudden movements. "Let's have that snack, okay?"

Maggie stood, her hand still on Joey's shoulder. "I have a great idea. You guys can take your cookies and milk in on the coffee table and watch that new Christmas video we bought. Sound good?"

Joey nodded, his face relaxing. "I get to turn it on." He ran toward the living room. The other two children emerged from the corner to follow him.

Anger rocketed through Grant. Was that what they normally did? Cowered in the corner to protect themselves from some adult who was supposed to be taking care of them?

He stalked to the window and stared out past the red geranium on the sill. Dusk was drawing in, seeping down the mountains to cloak the village in shadows.

Behind him, he heard Maggie carrying cookies and milk into the other room. He heard the music of the video start and sensed her return to the kitchen.

When he was sure he had control of himself, he

turned to face her, determined to keep his voice below the level of the video from the next room.

"Is that why the mother's not here? Because she abused them?"

He read the answer in the horrified expression on Maggie's face.

"Of course not! Nella's a good mother. She'd never do anything to hurt her children. In fact, she'd take—"

She stopped abruptly, but he knew the rest of it.

"She'd let him hit her rather than the kids." Tiredness laced his voice. He'd seen this way too many times in the E.R., and it still sickened him.

Maggie nodded, glanced toward the door, then stepped a little closer. "The best thing Ted Bascom ever did was wrap his truck around a tree. I don't think you'd find a soul in Button Gap to say any different."

"You're telling me people knew." His hands clenched. "Why didn't you do something about it, if you're all so concerned about each other here?"

She paled. "We tried. Don't you realize we'd try? None of the Bascoms would ever tell the truth about it. It was always how awkward Nella had been, or how she'd fallen down the steps yet again."

"You still should have called the police."

Maggie rubbed her arms as if chilled. "I did that once. It just made things worse. And the police couldn't do anything when Nella declared up and down that she'd just fallen and Ted wouldn't hurt her. He had her convinced she was nothing without him."

"Social services, then."

If anything, her face went even whiter. "There's no point in your telling me what we should have done. Believe me, we tried everything. I think I'd almost gotten Nella to the point of moving to a shelter when Ted's death made it unnecessary. Now we just have to help them put their lives back together again."

She was right. He knew as well as anyone how often well-meaning efforts failed.

"Sorry. I didn't mean to second-guess you. I know you've been going the extra mile for them."

He clasped her shoulder in what was meant to be a comforting gesture. He wasn't prepared for the overwhelming urge to draw her against him, to soothe away the distress in her eyes.

First the kids. Now Maggie. It seemed Button Gap was getting under his skin in more ways than one.

Could she trust Grant with the truth or couldn't she?

Maggie was still struggling with that question on Friday morning as she filled out yet another of the many forms the county insisted upon. Sometimes she thought the whole clinic would sink under an avalanche of useless paperwork.

The forms were the least of her concerns at the moment. She let her fingers rest over the computer keys and stared across the waiting room, empty at the moment.

The wide front window gave a gray view of a mostly deserted street. The west wind whipped the flag in front of the post office. It sent a stray newspaper fluttering along like a tumbleweed.

Winter—that was what it looked like. The gray sky suggested snow, and the few people who were out and about had bundled up in winter jackets and scarves. The weather, along with everything else, reminded her of the rapidly passing days. Soon it would be Christmas.

She pressed her fingers against the headache that had been building behind her eyes for the past day. Nella would return before Christmas, surely. She couldn't bear to miss the holiday with her children.

*If she doesn't,* a little voice whispered relentlessly in her ear, *if she doesn't, what will you do?*

*Well, I won't panic,* she retorted. *I'll find a way to deal with the situation.*

Which just brought her back to her original question. Could she trust Grant with the secret she hid?

She'd come close to telling him the day before. His sympathy, when he'd realized what Nella and the children had endured, had touched her to the heart. She'd been within a breath of pouring out everything.

Some instinctive caution had held her back. She massaged her temples with her fingertips. Certainly her life would be easier if Grant knew the truth, if he were part of the Button Gap conspiracy.

She didn't know him well enough to be sure of how he'd react. That was the bottom line. Each time she thought she had Grant figured out, he surprised her.

"What are you doing?"

Her hands jerked away from her head. "Nothing. That

is, I'm working on the latest statistics report the county office has decided to plague us with."

He nodded, leaning against the desk. "Bureaucrats. They're the same no matter where they are."

That was a featherweight in the balance toward telling him the truth. If he shared her distaste for those who quibbled while others tried to make a difference in people's lives, he might understand about Nella and the children.

She stretched, trying to cover her uncertainty. "We could use someone else in the office just to handle all the paperwork, but that's not going to happen."

"No, they like to keep you on a shoestring, don't they?" He bent a little closer. "How are the kids today? I hope Joey's not still upset."

She found herself turning toward him without really intending the movement. *Get a grip,* she told herself.

"He seems to be fine. Kids are remarkably resilient. At least, I keep telling myself that."

"It's hard to understand how a man could treat his own child that way." His mouth tightened. "As often as I've seen it, I still can't grasp it."

"They're safe now."

*He does understand. Surely it's all right to tell him.*

She looked up, the words hovering on her lips. But Grant wasn't looking at her any longer. He was staring past her at the computer screen.

"This can't be right." He pointed, frowning at one of the lines she'd filled in. "You've made a mistake."

"Not exactly." Her fingers clenched. She should have

closed that file the moment she realized he was standing behind her.

He transferred the frown to her. "What do you mean, 'not exactly'?"

"We've always reported the statistics that way. Doc Harriman figured out a long time ago that the county wouldn't cover the vitamins he ordered for the children if he filled it in as vitamins, so he—"

"Cheated." Grant's tone was uncompromising.

"It's not cheating! He just described it a little differently. If we don't do that, we can't give vitamins to the kids whose families can't afford to buy them. What's more important, a line on a form or a child's health?"

Grant pulled away from the desk and straightened. Every line of his body proclaimed that he didn't accept what she was saying.

"I don't care how you rationalize it, Maggie. It's not the right way. There are other programs that will cover the cost of vitamins."

"Not without pushing families to go through a lot of red tape. Some of them won't do it."

He didn't understand. She'd argued this out a hundred times with her own conscience, but had always come to the same conclusion—the children had to come first.

"That's not our responsibility. We follow the rules. To the letter. Understood?"

She swallowed the argument that wanted to burst out of her mouth and gave a reluctant nod. She understood.

She also understood the answer to the question that

had been plaguing her. She couldn't possibly confide in Grant about the Bascom kids.

He might sympathize with their plight, even understand what she was trying to do. But that wouldn't deter him. He'd go by the book. He'd turn them in.

So he couldn't know—ever.

## Chapter Six

"Quietly now. Dr. Grant is probably sleeping in, and we don't want to bother him." Maggie followed the children out the door Saturday morning.

Joey leaped off the porch with a shout, followed by Robby. Clearly it was futile to expect three healthy children to be quiet.

She took Tacey's hand and followed the boys, holding the ax close against her side. Actually, she was delighted to hear the Bascoms making noise. They'd been unnaturally quiet for so long that a little ordinary rambunctious behavior could only be a good thing.

This morning, though, she'd like to get well away from the house before Grant was stirring. In fact, she'd be happy if she didn't have to see him again until Monday morning.

Her stomach clenched as she pictured his face the day before when he'd talked about following the rules to the letter. He'd acted as if she were a thief.

The tightness in her stomach seemed to throb. Maybe that was how he saw her.

Well, Dr. Grant Hardesty didn't know everything, even if he thought he did. She beat down the little voice that whispered maybe he had a point.

She was only doing what she had to do to take care of her people. The next time she saw him, maybe she'd just tell him so.

"Good morning. Where are you off to so early?"

Grant stood on the back steps of his side of the house. She'd assumed he was safely in bed, but he looked as if he'd been up for hours, already dressed and shaved.

She swallowed, clearing her throat. But before she could answer, Robby did.

"A Christmas tree!" He bounced up and down, nearly bouncing out of the too-large boots she'd found for him. "We getting a Christmas tree."

It was the first time the four-year-old had voluntarily spoken to Grant. She supposed she should be happy.

"That's great." He glanced at Maggie, seeming to notice the ax, and lifted his eyebrows. "Imitating Paul Bunyan, are you?"

Amazing how that man could make her feel foolish with just a look. "Not exactly. We're going up to Jack White's woods to cut a tree. He offered us one."

Robby stopped at the bottom of the steps. "You wanna come?"

Robby had picked a great time to be friendly.

"I'm sure Dr. Grant has too many things to do today for that." She kept walking. "Come on, Robby."

"Actually, I don't have a thing to do." His voice stopped her. "Maybe I can help."

He'd probably volunteered just to be contrary. She turned slowly to face him.

"You don't need to do that. We can manage."

"But I'd like to. Don't you want me to come, Maggie?" The expression in his eyes told her he knew exactly what he was doing, and exactly what her answer would have to be.

"Fine." She tried not to let her voice reveal her feelings. "We'd be glad to have you."

No, they wouldn't be glad. *She* wouldn't, anyway. Quite aside from the awkward memory of yesterday's encounter, every moment that Grant was with the children was a moment when she had to be on guard. But she didn't have a choice. Making an issue of it would just raise his suspicions.

Grant fell into step beside her, the kids dancing ahead of them. They skirted adjoining backyards and headed for the lane, their feet crunching over frost-crisp grass.

"I'm really not trying to crash your party, Maggie."

A quick glance told her he was watching her with a faintly amused expression.

"Why did you, then?" She may as well be blunt. Nothing else seemed to work with him.

His amusement vanished. "Not from any burning desire for your company, believe me. I thought it would be good to show Joey I really am a friend, not a threat."

So much for being blunt. He'd thrown it right back at her and put her in the wrong, as well.

"I—" She couldn't think of anything she could say to excuse her rudeness. "I'm sorry. That's very thoughtful of you."

It was more than thoughtful. It showed a degree of perception she hadn't expected from him, and that put her off balance yet again.

"He's a nice kid." Grant sounded slightly surprised as he made the admission. "Given what he went through, I'd have expected more problems."

"Sometimes you can't see the damage." He couldn't know how deeply the subject cut for her.

He watched the kids, frowning just a little. "Isn't their mother due back soon? I thought you said she would be away only a few more days."

That's what she'd said, all right. "Yes, well, she had some family business to take care of."

Nella *had* gone back to the town where her family once lived. And what she was doing might be described as family business, after all. She was trying to find the courage to keep her family together. After years of being convinced she couldn't do anything without her husband, that was a tough battle.

"I hope it won't take much longer."

If there was a question in that, she'd prefer to ignore it. "I'm sure it won't." They'd reached the edge of town, and she waved toward the field that stretched toward the woods. "Up that way, Joey."

He nodded, waved and started off at a run through the frost-touched weeds. Tacey and Robby followed him.

Their jackets were bright splotches of crimson and blue against the silvered grass.

Grant put out his hand toward the ax. "I'll carry that for you."

Did he think she was helpless? "No." That came out a little harshly. "Thanks, anyway."

She could sense his gaze on her face as they crossed the brittle stubble, probing as if to question her every comment. She looked firmly away, concentrating instead on the way the slant of December sunlight picked out the blossoms of daisy fleabane and wild asters, dried on the stalk.

"You sound a little hoarse this morning." It was his cool professional tone. "Is your throat sore?"

She cleared her throat. She had no intention of turning into one of Dr. Hardesty's patients, although it would probably be impolite to tell him so.

"A bit scratchy, that's all." She pointed toward the plantation of evergreens dotting the hillside ahead of them. "There are the trees Jack mentioned. He said we could pick any one that's not marked."

The kids were already running between the trees, exclaiming about first one, then another. Grant pushed through a stand of dried goldenrod, its stems crackling. He paused to eye a slightly misshapen Scotch pine.

"Does he grow these for a living?"

She had to smile. "Doesn't look like much of a living, does it? A few years ago, half the county decided there was money to be made in Christmas trees. Anyone with a woodlot started planting them, without thinking about the cost of getting them to market."

"Not a successful experiment, I take it."

"Most of the trees ended up like this, trimmed for a few years, then left to go wild."

"We ought to be able to find one that's not too bad, especially if we trim off the bottom."

That was just what she'd been thinking, but she was surprised that had occurred to him. "I'm sure your Christmas tree is always perfectly shaped."

He shrugged. "The ones I remember as a kid always looked perfect by the time I saw them, anyway. My mother had them professionally decorated."

"Professionally decorated?" The concept boggled her mind. "You didn't trim your own Christmas tree?"

He frowned, then glanced toward the kids. "Hey, guys. Did any of you see one you like yet?"

Apparently she wasn't going to get an answer to that unguarded question. Well, fair enough. She'd certainly evaded plenty of his questions. But what kind of a childhood had Grant Hardesty had, anyway?

Tacey tugged gently at Grant's hand, then pointed. He looked down at her, his face softening.

"Did you find one you like? Show me."

Maggie followed as Tacey led the way past several scraggly pines. She stopped in front of a small blue spruce.

"This one," Tacey whispered. Her eyes seemed filled with stars as she looked up at it.

Joey, joining them, scowled. "I want one that goes clean to the roof. Me 'n' Robby want a big one."

"Believe me, this tree will look a lot bigger when you get it inside," Grant said.

Maggie knew that Tacey had just tugged on his heartstrings. She knew, because she felt the same.

"My ceilings are pretty low," she pointed out. "We don't want to have to cut the top off to get the tree in."

Joey looked unconvinced. She made a point of feeling the spruce's needles.

"I don't know, though. Blue spruce is pretty prickly. Your hands might not be tough enough to trim it."

Joey quickly grasped a branch in one bare fist. "That's nothing," he boasted. "I can trim this one easy as pie. Let's take it."

Over the children's heads, Grant's gaze met hers, softening in a smile. "I guess this is it, then."

Maggie hefted the ax. "Step back a bit."

"Let me," Grant said at almost the same moment.

"I can do it." Her grip tightened on the smooth wood of the handle.

"I'm sure you can."

Grant took a step closer, his body blocking out her view of the children. It was as if they were alone. He closed his hand over hers.

"I'm sure you can," he repeated, his voice lower. "But why should you? Do you dislike me so much that you won't even let me cut down a tree for you?"

*Dislike* definitely wasn't the right word, not with his

skin warm against hers and a hundred messages racing along her nerves straight to her heart.

"I don't dislike you." She was suddenly breathless, and she took a quick inhalation of cold, pine-scented air. She let go of the handle. "I'm just used to doing things for myself."

His eyes, bluer than the December sky, were serious, as if what they talked about was critically important. "It's good to be independent. But like the kids say, you should always share." He smiled then, taking the ax.

Her heart gave an erratic flutter. That wasn't his polite, professional, well-mannered smile. It was considerably more potent.

She took a careful step back. No, what she felt was definitely not dislike. What she felt could be a lot more dangerous than that.

Grant stood at the front window on Sunday, watching as a little parade composed of Maggie and the children crossed the street and entered the house. They'd stood on the corner for a few moments, talking with Aunt Elly. Then the damp chill in the air must have gotten to them, because they'd raced toward the door.

They'd been to church, obviously. It had looked as if everyone in Button Gap went to Sunday services. Everyone but him, that is.

Maybe going to church would have been better than staying in the dingy apartment on such a gray day.

No, probably not. He'd had enough reminders of his

grudge against God the night he'd attended the pageant rehearsal.

He toyed with the idea of taking off in the car. The terms of his servitude didn't require that he stay in Button Gap when he wasn't on duty.

But that would feel like running away—from his post, from the unwelcome thoughts of Maggie that had occupied him far too much in the past day.

He frowned out at the now-deserted street. Everyone had headed home for Sunday dinner, probably. A few flakes of snow drifted down from the leaden sky, then a few more.

Joey had been wishing for snow yesterday. He'd talked about it the whole time they were dragging the tree home. He wanted it to snow, and he wanted a new toboggan for his birthday next week.

Well, it looked as if he'd get the snow. As for the toboggan, maybe his mother was taking care of that. Or Maggie.

Every train of thought seemed to lead back to the same place. He turned away from the window, exasperated with himself.

All right, Maggie interested him. Or maybe disturbed him would be a better way of putting it. Admit it, and move on.

It was ridiculous that she was so unwilling to accept any help from anyone. Especially from him. Look how she'd behaved when he'd wanted to cut down the tree. He might have been a mugger, trying to wrest something valuable from her.

Maggie's prickly, determined personality wasn't one he could ever be serious about, but still, she intrigued him. He'd like to see her admit she needed help from someone once in a while.

But probably not from him. He opened the refrigerator door and stared with distaste at the meager contents. He wasn't going to be around long enough for Maggie to learn to depend on him. Another couple of weeks, and he'd be back to his normal life.

He settled for a can of soda, slid into the wobbly recliner and tilted back. He'd concentrate on planning the life he'd have once he returned to Baltimore and started his practice with Rawlins. He should look for a new apartment right away, given how hard it was to find something. Or maybe it was time to consider buying one of the renovated row houses down near the harbor.

By the time he'd finished the soda, the room had darkened so much that he could barely see. A glance out the window told him the reason. The snow had gone from flurries to a steady, dense fall. Already it frosted the shrubs and trees, giving Button Gap a soft, muted visage.

Maybe Joey should have specified how much snow he wanted. Grant reached out to switch on the lamp next to the chair. The bulb came on, then went off. Even as he frowned at it, it came back on again.

Okay, the electricity was flickering. He got up with a protesting squeal from the recliner. He'd better locate a flashlight, in case the power actually went off.

His hand had just closed over the flashlight in the

desk drawer when the lamp flickered again, then went out. He waited a moment. Nothing.

Well, all right. He switched on the flashlight. He'd be fine. Bored, but fine.

Then, slowly, his brain identified the grumbling thud he'd heard when the light went out. The furnace. Maggie had told him that the furnace motor was electric. Without electricity, he had no heat.

He was coming back from the bedroom, pulling on a sweater, when he heard someone pounding persistently at the back door. Tugging the sweater down, he opened the door.

Joey had come out without a coat, and he hopped up and down on the porch to keep warm. "Maggie says the 'lectricity is out. Maggie says come over to our place so you won't freeze."

An afternoon in close quarters with Maggie and the three kids. And a fireplace. And a wood burner.

Joey danced. "You comin' or not?"

It was better than freezing.

"You go on back. Tell Maggie I'll be along in a minute."

The apartment was already cooling. He picked up an armful of journals he hadn't had time to read yet. This wouldn't be so bad. Maggie would undoubtedly occupy the kids, and he could immerse himself in the journals. He could make decent use of the time.

Pulling on his jacket, he hurried outside, slamming the door behind him. A step off the porch took him to his shoe tops in snow. He strode across the yard behind the clinic to Maggie's kitchen door, gave a cursory knock and opened it.

"Maggie?"

"Come on in." The croak had to be Maggie's voice, but it sounded more like a frog.

He crossed to the living room doorway, shedding his jacket on the way. He paused.

Maggie sat on the braided rug in front of the fireplace, surrounded by Christmas ornaments and the three kids. The blue spruce they'd cut the previous day occupied the place of honor in front of the window. They'd clearly been spending their Sunday afternoon trimming it.

The room looked like Christmas. Bright cards decorated the top of the pine jelly cabinet in the corner, and a rather crooked red-and-green paper chain swung from the white window curtains.

Maggie didn't look as festive as the setting. She sneezed several times, then mopped her face with a tissue. Her eyes were about as red as her nose, and her usually glossy hair was disheveled.

"I said you were catching something, didn't I?" He picked his way through the boxes scattered on the braided rug to reach her. "Do you have a fever?"

She evaded his hand. "No. It's just a cold."

He touched her cheek. "And a fever. And a sore throat. What have you taken?"

"Nothing." At his look, she went defensive. "I can't take something that will make me sleepy, not when I have the children to take care of."

He glanced at the kids. They stood close together,

eyes wary, obviously not sure what to do when Maggie, always strong Maggie, wasn't herself.

"I'll watch the kids. You need to take something right now and get some sleep."

*He'd* watch the kids? Where did that come from?

Maggie apparently found the suggestion just as incredible. "I'll be fine."

He grabbed her arms and hoisted her to her feet, surprised by how light she was. Maybe her assertive attitude made her seem bigger than she was. He guided her to the couch.

"You won't be fine unless you follow doctor's orders. Do you have something to take, or do I have to go over to the clinic?"

Maggie sank down on the couch, apparently too sick to argue. That alarmed him more than anything.

"Top shelf above the sink in the kitchen," she murmured.

He found the vial, nodded his approval and raided the refrigerator for juice. He went back to the living room to find her curled up, eyes half-closed.

"Here." He stood over her while she downed the pills he doled out, then handed her a glass of juice. "Drink that and relax for a while."

She nodded, tucking her hand under the bright pillow with a little sigh.

He turned to the kids, to find they were all looking at him. A flicker of panic touched him. He couldn't suggest they watch television, not without electricity. What was he going to do with them?

"Why don't you guys sit down by the fireplace and… um, play a game."

Joey shook his head with a look of disgust. "We don't want to play any old game. We want to finish trimming the Christmas tree."

A voice seemed to echo over the years. Jason's voice. *Don't you wish we had a Christmas tree of our very own, Grant? One we could trim ourselves?*

He swung toward Maggie, ready to demand she get well and take over.

Maggie slept, her flushed cheek pressed against the patchwork pillow that he'd bet Aunt Elly had made for her. Silky dark hair swung across her face, and one blue-jeaned leg dangled from the couch.

He lifted her leg to the couch, moved the orange juice glass and brushed a strand of hair back from her face. It flowed through his fingers damply, clinging.

A patchwork quilt draped over the back of the couch. He pulled the quilt free, then tucked it around her, moving with the utmost care so he wouldn't wake her. Finally, satisfied that she was comfortable, he turned back to the kids.

He didn't want to do this. But Maggie needed him.

"So, what do you say we finish trimming this Christmas tree?"

Maggie woke reluctantly from a dream in which she had been warm and safe—a child snug in a soft bed, tucked in with love and kisses.

She blinked, coming back to the present. Firelight—

yes, the power was off. The room was warm, and the murmur of voices must have made the background music for her dream.

She sniffed, not stirring. Someone must have been cooking on the wood burner. Maybe Aunt Elly had taken over while she was sleeping.

Still reluctant to move, she snuggled under the quilt. Someone had covered her. Someone had tucked her in and told her to sleep. Grant.

She looked toward the fireplace.

Grant sat on the rug in front of the fire, Tacey on his lap, Robby leaning against his knee, Joey sitting cross-legged holding her big yellow mixing bowl filled with popcorn. The old metal popcorn popper she used for camping was propped against the stone fireplace.

"...so Jack and his mother lived happily ever after. The end."

If someone had told her yesterday that Dr. Grant Hardesty would be telling fairy tales to the Bascom kids on her living room rug, she'd have thought they were lying. But this was definitely Grant, even though his face looked softer, somehow, with the firelight flickering on it.

Tacey reached up to tug at Grant's sweater. "A Christmas story," she said softly.

"Yeah, tell us a Christmas story," Joey chipped in. He shoved a handful of popcorn in his mouth.

She wasn't imagining the shadow that crossed Grant's face at that request. Something about Christmas disturbed him at a level so deep, he probably never let it show. Did he admit it to himself?

He ruffled Joey's hair, and for once the boy didn't duck away from a touch. "Why don't we—" He glanced across the room and saw she was awake. "Why don't we see if Maggie needs anything, okay?"

She roused herself to push the quilt back. Those children were her responsibility, and she'd been sound asleep, leaving them to Grant.

"Sorry I slept so long. I'll get up and—"

Grant was there before she could get off the couch. He shoved her gently back to a sitting position on the couch. "No, you won't do any such thing."

She'd have taken offense at the order, but it was said with such concern that she couldn't. It must be the cold that made her feel so tearful. "I'm sorry. I shouldn't have left you with the kids."

He raised an eyebrow even as he touched her cheek and then felt her pulse. "Don't you think I can manage three kids, a power outage and a snowstorm?"

Her gaze tangled with his, and her breath caught. "I think you can manage just about anything you set your mind to."

Joey leaned against the couch and eyed her critically. "You look some better, Maggie."

"Thanks." Although with Grant's fingers on her wrist, her pulse was probably racing. "You guys behaving?"

He looked affronted. "O' course we are. Grant made popcorn."

"A little fast," Grant murmured, and he let go of her hand.

She felt the heat rise in her cheeks. "I'm feeling much better. I didn't realize you could cook."

"Hey, if you want popcorn or soup, I'm your man." He straightened, stretching. "We kept some chicken soup warm for you. You feel as if you can eat some?"

She started to get up and was pushed back again.

"Sit still. Tacey and I are in charge of serving, aren't we, Tacey?"

The little girl actually giggled. Then she nodded and raced to the kitchen. It looked as if Grant had made a conquest.

Of Tacey, she reminded herself quickly. Not of her.

Something remarkably like panic ripped along her nerves, pulling her upright. She couldn't let a momentary gentleness and an afternoon's support make her feel anything for Grant. She wouldn't. That could only lead to heartbreak.

## *Chapter Seven*

Grant shoved another log on the fire and watched as Maggie tucked blankets around the sleeping children. After several stories and snacks, the kids had finally curled up in the nests of blankets she'd created on the living room rug. Thanks to a busy afternoon the tree was trimmed and the ornament boxes put away.

Maggie looked better, and she had things under control. He ought to go back to his own place.

Instead of moving, he settled comfortably into the spot on the braided rug he'd occupied for the past hour, his back against the couch. He stretched out his legs toward the fire.

The power was still off. His apartment would be cold. Maggie might need something.

Those sounded like good enough reasons for staying right where he was.

Maggie glanced out the window at the snowy darkness, then came and sat down next to him. The flush in her cheeks looked natural now, rather than fever-caused.

He put the backs of his fingers against her cheek, just to be sure. Her skin was warm and smooth.

"You okay?" He kept his voice low, although he didn't think anything short of an explosion would wake the kids now.

"Fine." She withdrew a fraction of an inch. "Would you believe it's still snowing out? I'd guess we'll have close to two feet by the time it's done."

"Probably just raining in Baltimore."

She settled back against the couch. "I'll take snow anytime. Maybe we'll have a white Christmas."

*Christmas.* The holiday was as unavoidable here as it was everywhere else this time of year. A flare of resentment went through him. Why did he have to be reminded?

Maggie seemed to take his silence for assent. She stared into the fire, apparently content for once to sit and watch instead of doing something.

She tilted her head, looking at the battered metal star he'd placed on the very top of the tree. "It looks nice, doesn't it?"

He assessed the spruce. The branches were crooked, and the top tilted a little oddly in spite of his best efforts to straighten it. Half the ornaments were old and worn, the other half homemade.

"Nice," he agreed.

She shot him a look, as if he'd argued about it. "I

know it can't compare to a decorator-trimmed tree, but I think it's pretty good."

His brother would have loved the tree, right down to the angels made from paper plates and glitter. The thought of Jason's reaction stabbed him to the heart.

"You have a beautiful tree, Maggie." The thing to do was keep the focus on Maggie and her Christmas, not his. That way was safe. "The kids are crazy about it."

"They are, aren't they?" She smiled in their direction, then got up. "I forgot one ornament."

She took a small box from the mantel, then opened it and removed something. For a moment she held the object protectively between her hands, and then she lifted it so he could see.

A fragile glass angel dangled from her fingers, the flickering light from the fire turning the wings to gold. The way she looked at the angel told him it had a special significance for her.

He got to his feet to look more closely. "Very pretty. It looks old."

"It was my mother's." Emotion shadowed her eyes. "The only thing I have left that was hers."

He touched one wing with a fingertip. "There's a little chip out. If the piece is in the box, maybe I could glue it in place."

"No." Something suddenly pained her face. "I don't have the piece. It was broken a long time ago."

"What happened?" The question was out before he considered that she might find it intrusive.

She shrugged, turning away to hang the angel from a high branch, safe from little hands, he supposed.

"Just an accident."

It must have been more than that, or she wouldn't have that shadow on her face when she looked at the angel's wing. But she clearly didn't intend to share the story with him.

Maggie bent over the enameled coffeepot that she'd put next to the fire to stay warm. "Ready for some more hot chocolate?"

"Sure, why not?" He picked up the mug he'd been using and held it out for a refill. He didn't have the right to push for answers she didn't want to give. He sat back down, letting her choose another subject.

She glanced toward the window again as she joined him on the floor. "I just hope the snow won't keep everyone home from pageant practice this week."

A safe enough subject, he supposed. "How is the pageant coming along? No more disputes about the magi?"

"No." She smiled. "But Pastor Jim used your comments about the magi in his sermon this morning. He said he wanted people to actually listen to the story instead of thinking they know it already."

Being quoted in a sermon had to be a first for him. "I wish I'd heard him."

"You could have come to church."

It blindsided him, coming on the heels of a casual comment he hadn't really meant. He didn't let his expression change, but she probably felt his tension.

"I could have. I didn't."

Let her make of that what she would. She'd probably get defensive. He didn't care. His private quarrel with God wasn't her concern.

"I hope you'll come on Christmas Eve for the pageant. The children would like that."

He couldn't detect anything critical in her voice, but she still might be thinking it.

"Maybe." He made his tone noncommittal. "If I'm still here."

He wouldn't be. His term of service was up that day. He'd be on the road back to his real life by the time the kids began to sing, letting Maggie and Button Gap recede in his rearview mirror and his memory.

What had possessed her to push him on that subject? Maggie could feel Grant's tension through the arm that brushed against hers. The moment she'd mentioned church, he'd withdrawn.

Well, he'd already made it fairly clear that church wasn't one of his priorities. And that it wasn't any of her business.

Besides, she didn't even want him to stay for the pageant. The sooner Grant left Button Gap, the sooner she could relax and get her life back to normal.

It was definitely time for a change of subject. Past time, really.

"Speaking of holidays, is Joey getting the toboggan he wants for his birthday?" Grant must have been thinking the same thing she was. He nodded toward the window. "Looks as if he'll have plenty of chances to use it."

She glanced at Joey, sprawled on his quilt, his fine blond hair almost white in the dim light. He looked defenseless in sleep, the way a child should.

"I managed to get a snow saucer for him from the church rummage sale. Once I've painted it, it'll be fine." Grant had probably never had a used present in his life, but Joey would appreciate it. "I'm afraid he'll have to share with the other two, though. They only had the one."

"I thought maybe his mother—"

Her hands, clasped loosely around her knees, gripped each other. "Nella can't afford a toboggan."

"Will she be back by Joey's birthday?"

"If she can be."

*Lord, please bring Nella home by then. Let her see how much the children need her. Give her strength.*

For a moment the silence stretched between them, broken only by the hiss and crackle of the fire. It was oddly comfortable, in spite of the awkward moments.

Well, Grant had things he didn't want to talk about, and she had her own secrets to hide. As long as they respected each other's boundaries, they could be—

That thought then led to a question. Friends? She wasn't sure that best described their relationship. Colleagues, maybe. At least they didn't have to be adversaries, did they?

Grant shifted, propping one elbow on his knee. In his

jeans and white sweater, he should have looked casually at home, but an indefinable something set him apart.

"So tell me, Maggie. What was it like, growing up here in Button Gap?"

She shrugged, thinking of all the things she wouldn't say to him about her childhood. "About like it is now. Small, isolated. Everyone knew everyone else."

"You lived right here in town?"

"No." Her fingers tightened as the image of the old farmhouse flashed into her mind, and she forced them to relax. "We lived out of town a couple of miles."

"So you rode the bus to school."

"Yes." When she came. When her father wasn't ranting about the uselessness of educating girls to think they were better than they were.

Grant lifted an eyebrow. "Would you like me to start paying you per word?"

"Sorry." She forced a smile. She'd learned ways of talking about the past that evaded the truth, that made it sound as if she'd had a childhood just like other kids. Why was it so hard to come up with the familiar fantasy for Grant? "Guess I'm just tired."

"Do you want to stretch out on the couch?"

He started to move, but she stopped him with a hand on his arm.

"No, I'm fine." She spread her hands, palms up. "There's not much to tell. I always wanted to be a nurse, but there wasn't enough money for college. So I went to Hagerstown, where I could get a decent job. I took classes at the community college."

"In a nursing degree program?"

"I planned to get into an LPN program. That was all I could afford. But some people at the church I went to took an interest in me. They helped me get scholarship money and made it possible to go for an R.N. instead."

"It sounds as if they were friends."

She nodded, thinking of the college professor and his wife who'd practically adopted her, of the young family who'd given her room and board in exchange for baby-sitting, of the elderly woman who'd paid her tuition when she couldn't possibly have gone to school otherwise.

"They were good friends." Her throat tightened. "I owe them a great deal."

"I'm sure you repaid them when you could."

She shook her head, getting a lump in her throat at the thought of their responses.

"I tried to. They all said the same thing. 'Use that degree to do good.' That's all they wanted."

"So you came back to Button Gap and did just that." He smiled, his eyes warm with what she might almost imagine was admiration. "I suspect those people are proud of you."

Grant's warmth drew her closer, like a flower turning toward the sun. He was only inches away in the quiet room, and the firelight flickered on his strong features and gilded his skin.

She took a breath, feeling as if she hadn't bothered to do that for several minutes.

"That's my story." She cleared her throat. "What about you?"

"How did I end up a doctor, you mean?"

She nodded. *Come on, Grant. Talk about something, anything, that's neutral enough to let me get my balance.*

"Was your father a doctor?"

He made a sound that might have been a laugh if it had had any humor in it. "That's not very likely. My father lives and breathes business. His company is all that interests him."

"I suppose he wanted you to go into business with him, then."

"That was the plan." His lips tightened. "When I decided to take premed, he persuaded himself it was a momentary lapse. I'd grow up and get over it. When I applied to medical school instead of Harvard Business School, the explosion could be heard up and down the eastern seaboard."

"Obviously you got your way." There was more tension in him than she'd have expected over a quarrel with his father that must have taken place several years earlier.

He shrugged. "There wasn't anything he could do to stop me. I had my own money."

The simple sentence defined the difference between them. He'd had his own money. Doors to the life he'd wanted had opened to him, because he'd been able to pay. Could he even imagine what life was like without that?

"Have you and your father made up?"

He tilted his head in a slight nod. "I guess so. We were never close, and that hasn't changed. Maybe he still expects me to walk into his office and take my rightful place at some point. It won't happen."

"No. You already have a partnership waiting for you, don't you?"

"I hope I do." He looked at her, a question in eyes that looked more green than blue in the dim light. "That's the life I want. Is something wrong with that?"

"I wasn't being critical." At least, she hoped she wasn't. "It sounds like a great opportunity. You'll be doing good work."

His smile broke through again. "It's not in a league with Button Gap, I admit. No one there will bring me apple butter in exchange for an office visit." His voice was gently teasing, and he leaned closer.

Did he realize how close he was? She could see the flecks of gold and hazel in his eyes, almost count the fine lines around his mouth.

"You'll miss that," she managed to say.

"That's not the only thing I'll miss," he said softly. And then his lips closed over hers.

For one second she almost believed she could pull back. Then her heart stirred and she melted against him, returning kiss for kiss. She touched his cheek, feeling the faint stubble of beard, the high cheekbone, the curve of his brow. It was as if she'd already memorized how his face would feel and only needed to touch it in confirmation.

His lips moved to her cheek, and he traced a line of soft kisses. "Maggie."

The sound of her name seemed to bring her back

to herself. Slowly, carefully, she drew away. Her heart thudded, and her breath came as if she'd been running. Firelight still flickered, the children still slept. Everything in the room was the same.

Except her.

She wanted to make light of it, wanted to say it was nothing, just a kiss, but she couldn't. Even now, the weakness seemed to permeate her very bones.

Weakness. She couldn't be weak. She could never be weak.

She straightened, leaned back, tried to find a way to meet his gaze that wouldn't betray the fact that he'd cut right through all her defenses as if they were butter.

Grant looked at her with a question in his eyes, as if leaving it to her to say how they would respond to this.

"I don't think that was a good idea." She tried for a light touch and feared she failed.

"Right." He pulled back an inch or two, his smile chilling to something impersonal. "We have to work together. No sense complicating things."

That was what she thought herself, so why did it bother her so much when he put it into words? She tried to get her wits about her. This was for the best.

"You'll be leaving Button Gap before long, anyway."

"Speaking of leaving—" he glanced at his watch, then got to his feet "—I think it's time I went home."

"You don't have to go just because—" *Just because you kissed me.* "The power might not come back on for hours."

He shrugged into his jacket. "I'll be fine. A little cold

air might be just the thing right now." A few strides took him to the door, and then he paused. "Don't worry about it, Maggie. It was just the firelight."

She nodded, pinning a smile on her face as he went out into the dark.

*Just the firelight.* She'd like to believe that. She really would.

Grant paused in the clinic's hallway, studying the chart for the next patient. Unfortunately he wasn't exactly thinking about the patient. Maggie's face kept imposing itself on the medical form, looking the way he'd seen it the previous evening with her eyes dark in the firelight.

He'd kissed her. No big deal. It had been a temporary aberration, brought on by the situation. In the cold light of day, they were both quite ready to forget it ever happened.

Something else had come out of their enforced, snowbound isolation. He and Maggie knew each other considerably better than they had before it happened. He wasn't sure yet whether that was good or bad.

He glanced toward the desk, where Maggie was leaning over the counter to talk with someone in the waiting room. She'd had to go through a lot to become a nurse. That protectiveness of hers was an asset, and so was her fierce determination. She'd probably never have succeeded without those qualities.

As for the faith that came through in every aspect of her life—well, it was one more barrier between them.

If the God he'd once trusted did indeed exist, He'd have to be satisfied with Grant devoting his life to healing, because that was all he had to offer.

The bottom line was that he'd learned to respect Maggie, even to want her friendship. But it was just as well that they both understood anything else was out of the question. He pushed open the exam room door and put her firmly out of his mind.

Three patients later, he was checking out an elderly man with chronic bronchitis when the exam room door flew open.

"We have an emergency out in the woods." Before he could react, Maggie was handing him his jacket. "We have to go now."

"Wait a second." He frowned. "What kind of emergency? I'm in the middle of seeing a patient."

Maggie gave the elderly man a quick smile. "Harold understands, don't you, Harold?"

The patient was already sliding off the exam table and reaching for his shirt. "Sure thing, Maggie. You folks go on. I'll see the doc later."

As soon as he'd cleared the door, Maggie began filling a bag with supplies.

"The call just came in. A logger, badly hurt, out near Boone's Hollow. The helicopter can't land anywhere near them, so we'll have to go."

"Any idea of the type of injuries?" He pulled the jacket on, automatically double-checking the equipment she was packing.

She shook her head. "His partner called, badly

shaken. Thank goodness for cell phones. It sounds as if his leg is trapped, and he's bleeding heavily. I gave them emergency instructions before I lost the signal."

Maggie's face was grim, and every move was swift and efficient. She'd undoubtedly done this before.

By the time they reached the waiting room, it was already clearing out.

"I'll lock up," one woman offered. Her face was vaguely familiar. One of the pie bakers from the pageant rehearsal, he thought.

"Thanks, Mavis." Maggie just kept moving, apparently confident the woman would handle things.

"I'll start the prayer chain," the woman added. She touched his arm as he went by. "Good luck, Doc." It was oddly like a blessing.

Outside, he started automatically toward his vehicle, but Maggie was already yanking open the door of her battered truck instead.

"We can take mine—" he began, but she shook her head as she stowed the bag behind the seat.

"You don't want to get yours all scratched up, even if it could make it." She patted a dented fender. "She might not look pretty, but she'll get us there."

She slid behind the steering wheel.

He suppressed the automatic desire to question her decision. Maggie knew the way, presumably, and he didn't. He was on her turf. He climbed in next to her.

Maggie took off down the still-slushy street, then turned onto the road that went up the mountain. In just a few minutes the dense woods closed in on them on both sides of the snow-covered road.

Road? Grant braced himself with one hand against the dash as the truck hit a rut. It was hardly more than a track.

He glanced at Maggie. "Sure you know the way?"

She nodded, eyes narrowed as she searched the road ahead. "I used to live in this area. I know every foot of it."

Weak sunshine had melted most of the snow from the streets in the village, but here the mountain loomed over them, casting its perennial shadow. Hemlock branches bowed down with snow slapped the sides of the truck, as if intent on keeping them out. He had a sense of entering a bleak, unforgiving and very alien world.

Nonsense. He shook off the thought. This was an emergency call, nothing more. It hadn't occurred to him that he'd be doing this, but it should have. Out here, they were the first line of medical defense. He looked again at Maggie, and she seemed to feel his gaze.

"What?"

"Nothing." Then, as they slid around a bend, he realized that wasn't true. There was something. "You were right about the truck. You're much more capable of driving this than I am."

The expression in her eyes told him how surprised she was at his admission. Had he really been so arrogant that she thought him incapable of admitting it when he was wrong?

The road narrowed still more, so that the truck

seemed to force its way through the overhanging branches. He spotted a broken mailbox tilting listlessly on a post by a lane that was nothing more than a thread through the forest. Davis, it read in faded letters.

"That was where you lived?"

She nodded, her jaw tight with tension. "About a mile hike back."

He whistled. "Your parents must have liked their privacy."

"My father did." She clamped her mouth shut on the words.

He had just enough time to wonder if she'd ever tell him what it was about her past that pained her so when she turned in by another mailbox.

"We're almost there. The patient is Jake Riley, about forty, good general health, no existing conditions to worry about. His wife said she'd post the boy by the lane to show us where they are."

Even as the words were out of her mouth, he spotted the small figure ahead of them, waving. Grant grabbed the medical bag and slid out as Maggie pulled to a stop.

She was by his side almost before his feet hit the ground, it seemed. "Where are they?"

The boy, his face tearstained, pointed to a thick growth of woods. "That way. Hurry. You gotta hurry!"

Grant started toward the trees, adrenaline pumping, his legs churning through the heavy snow. Maggie was right beside him, keeping pace with him. He had a moment's thought for the probable reaction of his hospital colleagues if he tried to describe the situation.

They wouldn't believe it. He hardly believed it himself, but one thing he recognized. He could count on Maggie without question, without doubt. Whatever awaited them, she wouldn't let him down.

## Chapter Eight

Blades whirling, the Life Flight helicopter lifted off, carrying the patient to the hospital where a surgical team waited. Maggie tilted her head back to watch it clear the trees, smiling at the spontaneous round of applause from those who watched from the ground.

*Thank You, Lord. Thank You.*

"He's going to be fine now." Grant held the wife's hands in both of his, his tone reassuring. "Don't worry. They'll take good care of him."

The woman murmured incoherent thanks, then walked away with the neighbor who was driving her to the hospital. The rest of the small group moved, in ones and twos, toward the trucks and snowmobiles that had brought them.

Grant stood watching them for a moment, his expression bemused.

"Where did they all come from?" He nodded toward the plow driver who'd cleared enough space for the helicopter to land. "I thought we were alone in the most desolate place on the planet. Suddenly people appeared out of nowhere."

*We're never alone.* She wanted to say the words aloud, but she wouldn't, not given the way Grant tensed whenever the subject of faith came up.

"Word spreads fast when someone needs help," she said instead. "One person calls another, he calls another. Anyone who can help just comes."

"In the city, we'd rely on the professionals in a situation like this."

She wasn't sure whether that was an oblique criticism or a compliment. Maybe it was just a statement of fact.

"We're the only professionals out here." She leaned against the truck. "Everyone else helps because they're needed, I guess. Because they know people would do the same for them."

She stamped her feet, feeling the cold for the first time in the past hour. She'd been too busy to notice, but now it seeped through her boots and invaded the space between her hat and her collar.

"We owe them a vote of thanks." Grant raised his hand as a truck spun by them. "He might not have made it without their help."

She looked at him, noting the pinched lines around his mouth and the strain in his eyes.

"He definitely wouldn't have made it without you." A shiver went through her. It had been a close thing, a very close thing. "I couldn't have done it. If you hadn't been here, we'd have lost him."

He caught her mittened hand in a strong grip and held

it for a moment. "I wouldn't be so sure of that. You did a good job, Maggie."

"Thanks." Suddenly she didn't feel quite so cold.

She climbed into the truck and started the motor, cranking the heater on all the way. Grant settled next to her, rubbing his hands together as if they'd never be warm. She watched as the last vehicle spun away, then pulled onto the road.

She could feel Grant's gaze on her face.

"I meant that, you know. You're a good nurse."

Most of the time she didn't even think to question that. It was who she was. But sometimes, it felt good to hear it from someone else.

"Thanks." She darted a sideways glance at him. "I meant what I said, too. Your skill saved him."

And his determination. She'd already known Grant was a skilled doctor. She just hadn't seen that fierce will of his brought to bear. He wouldn't *let* the patient slip away. That glimpse into his soul had startled and moved her.

He pulled his gloves off and held his hands out to the warm air streaming from the heater. "Let's just say we can all be proud of what we did today."

She *was* proud—of her people, who'd done just what she'd known they'd do. Of Grant, who'd shown her a passion she hadn't expected.

She took the turn onto the main road. The snow was melting from it now, leaving bare ruts where other vehicles had gone. It was only early afternoon. The whole episode had taken less than two hours, but it felt like a lifetime since they'd raced out of the clinic.

"Okay," she said. "We all did a good job. But if what you did today was the only thing you accomplished during your month here, it would be enough."

His face relaxed in a smile. "We make a good team."

The words repeated themselves in her mind as she drove the rest of the way to the village. *A good team.*

She'd like to believe she and Grant were a team, but she knew better. Still, if she could ever care enough about someone to risk marriage, it would have to be with someone who would treat her as a partner. Someone who could respect her independence because he didn't doubt his own strength. Someone like Grant.

Not Grant, she told herself quickly. That was out of the question. But someone like him.

*Why not him?* A little voice whispered the question in her mind. *Why not Grant?*

She knew the answer to that one. It would never work. They'd both recognized that flare of attraction between them, and they'd both seen that it had to be extinguished.

Well, no. If she were being honest, she'd have to say she hadn't succeeded in extinguishing it. Not when she still felt a little flutter in her heart at the brush of his hands and the curve of his smile.

Controlled, then, she told herself firmly, and tried to ignore the faint flicker of hope that teased her heart and refused to go away.

Grant pulled his jacket on, fighting the strong inclination to flop down in the recliner and zip aimlessly through the channels. He hadn't realized how tired he was until after they'd treated the string of patients who'd had to be put off for the emergency run.

He zipped his jacket and glanced into the refrigerator. Everything. He was out of everything. That was why he was about to trek to the store instead of relaxing after the long day.

It had been long, but also very satisfying. They'd done good work, he and Maggie. As he'd told her, they made a good team.

Nevertheless, he absolutely wouldn't let himself think of Maggie in any terms but professional. They were colleagues. Nothing more. He might have given in to temptation for one kiss, but he wouldn't make that mistake again. It wasn't fair to either of them.

The kids were making a racket in the backyard. He grabbed his car keys, swung the door open and took a snowball right in the chest.

The action in the snow-covered yard froze. Maggie, bundled up in that red anorak that made her look like a cardinal, seemed almost as horrified as Joey. The kid's expression was so guilty that it was clear who'd thrown the snowball.

It hurt his heart to see the fear mixed with the guilt in the boy's face. He had to find a way to wipe that out.

He shoved his keys into his pocket and grabbed a handful of snow from the porch railing. "You want a battle, do you?" He packed the ball and threw it, and snow splattered on Joey's shoulder.

Fear faded, and the kid grinned. "You call that a

snowball? Where'd you learn how to make snowballs, anyway?"

"It doesn't snow in Baltimore." Maggie rounded a snowball in her bare hands. "Not much, anyway. He hasn't had enough practice. We'll have to show him some snowballs."

"Yeah, show him." Joey scooped up snow, while Tacey and Robby watched, hanging back a little.

"Don't you dare." He gave Maggie a mock-fierce glare. "Just put that snowball down and step away from it."

She wiggled it in her fingers. "Want it? Come and get it."

He charged, taking the snowball in the face and shaking it off as he grabbed her. "For that, you get your face washed with snow."

"Get him." Joey ran at him, pitching his snowball and bending to scoop up more snow to toss.

In an instant, all three kids were pelting him with snow, their shyness forgotten. Ducking, laughing, he managed to grab a handful. He clung tight to Maggie's sleeve as she struggled to break free and managed to get some snow right in her face before she returned the favor.

Breathless, he mopped snow from his eyes, then realized he was holding her too close. Her face was inches from his, her dark eyes bright with laughter, her cheeks flushed. He wanted to kiss her. Again.

He let her go, turning to chase Joey across the yard.

But he'd better stop kidding himself that resisting the temptation was going to be easy.

"Enough," Maggie called, laughing as he rolled Joey in a snowdrift, tickling him. "Let's use all this energy to make our snowman and let Dr. Grant get back to whatever he was going to do."

"You wanna make a snowman with us, don't you?" Joey dusted himself off. "It's gonna be the biggest one ever."

He ought to go to the store, get some groceries and watch the news. But his tiredness had miraculously vanished, and he wanted to play in the snow.

"You bet," he said.

Maggie's glance was questioning. "Are you sure about this? You must be tired after the day we put in."

"You, too. But you're doing it." He bent, packing a snowball and rolling it through the deep, soft snow. "Besides, I'm out of practice."

Tacey scurried to help him roll the ball. "Didn't you used to make snowmen when you were little?"

That was probably the most she'd ever said to him, and he discovered that it gave him pleasure to think she considered him safe.

"Well, like Maggie said, it doesn't snow very much in Baltimore, where I grew up."

Her little face wrinkled in a frown. "Why not?"

"Well, it's close to the ocean." Meteorology had never been one of his best subjects. "It's not up high, like we are here in the mountains. We get a little bit of snow, but not usually enough to make snowmen."

"But didn't you ever get to?" Her mournful expression said that she thought he'd been deprived.

He scoured his memory. Suddenly a scene popped up, as clear and bright as if it had happened yesterday.

"I remember one time that I did." He looked down at Tacey, but instead of her face, he saw Jason's. "It was an unusual storm. They'd predicted rain, but it snowed and snowed. My little brother and I got off school because of it, and we decided to build a snowman."

"I didn't know you had a brother." Maggie dusted snow from her red mittens.

He felt the familiar tightening inside him, felt the urge to shut all the doors on his memories and pretend he hadn't said anything.

But that wouldn't be fair to the little girl, who'd brought it up quite innocently. Or to Maggie, who was just expressing interest in him.

"He was two years younger than I am. Jason." After so many years of not saying it, the name felt strange coming out of his mouth.

Maggie got the implication of the verb tense he'd used. He saw the recognition in her eyes.

"You and Jason made a snowman," Tacey prompted. "Was it a big, big snowman?"

"Well, it was pretty big." He measured with his hand. "About this high. Why don't we see if we can make one that big today?"

"We can do it," Joey said quickly. "I'll make this ball really big to go on the bottom." He scuffed through the trampled snow, rolling the ball ahead of him. The other two children ran to help him.

"I'm sorry," Maggie said softly. "I didn't know."

He wasn't surprised at her expression of sympathy. He *was* surprised at the overwhelming urge he had to pour out the whole story.

*Do you want to know why I'm angry at God, Maggie? Do you want to hear about a sweet, loving child who didn't have a chance to grow up?*

The thoughts burned in his mind. It would be a relief to say them, to let them pour out in a corrosive flood.

But he wouldn't. Saying those things would take his friendship with Maggie to a whole new plane, and it was a place where he never intended to go. Not with Maggie. Not with anyone.

"We'd better help the kids. That's getting too big for them to push."

Maggie nodded, accepting without words that he'd put the subject off-limits. She ran toward the children, her jacket a bright crimson splash against a white backdrop.

He followed. What on earth had possessed him to let his guard down so far? Button Gap seemed to be turning his life upside down.

Maybe it wasn't just Button Gap. Maybe it was Maggie.


"Seems like you're pretty taken with the new doc." Aunt Elly leaned against the kitchen counter the next morning and gave Maggie that look that probed to the bottom of her soul.

"I don't know what you mean." That sounded feeble, even to her. She didn't want to talk about Grant—didn't want to think about how deep her feelings for him might be.

"Oh, I 'spect you do, but if you don't want to talk yet, I'll leave it be."

Maggie shrugged into her jacket. "I'd better get to the office. You sure you don't mind staying with the children this morning?"

"You know I don't." Aunt Elly gave the oatmeal she was cooking another stir, filling the kitchen with such a warm, homey smell that Maggie wanted to sit back down instead of stepping out into the cold. "But, Maggie, how long are you going to go on taking care of those young'uns? Nella should be coming back here by this time."

Maggie paused, hand on the doorknob. As usual, Aunt Elly went right to the heart of the matter. "I thought she'd be back by now." She looked at the older woman, troubled. "I talked to her when she called the kids last night. Asked her. All she could do was cry."

Aunt Elly shook her head, tears filling her eyes. "Poor child. That man beat her down, all right. I know you figure she ought to come back on her own, but maybe that's not going to happen. Maybe you'll have to go after her. You've got a pretty good idea where she is, don't you?"

"I think I do, but I could be wrong." She rubbed

her forehead, feeling the tension that took up residence whenever she thought of Nella. "I keep going over and over it, trying to see the best thing to do. If I go after her, I'm afraid she'll never really be sure she'd have come back on her own. Besides, what excuse could I give Grant for taking off?"

"Maybe it's time you told that man the truth."

Maggie suspected her heart was in her eyes. "I don't know. I just don't know."

"Surely you can't think he'd give those children away—not now that he knows them."

"I want to believe he'd understand. I think he can be trusted. But what if I'm wrong? I can't let them be hurt because of my mistake."

Aunt Elly rubbed her hands on her apron. "I know. I know. Well, I'll pray about it. Maybe God has an answer for you about that."

"I hope so." She enveloped the older woman in a quick, strong hug, warmed as always by the feel of Aunt Elly's wiry arms around her. "I'd better go."

She crossed the frosty yard, pausing to smile at the snowman they'd made the day before. She'd provided the carrot and the scarf, but Grant had contributed the Orioles baseball cap the snowman wore instead of a top hat.

The man who'd played in the snow with the children wouldn't turn them in to the authorities. He couldn't. Could he?

Pricked by her unaccustomed indecision, she walked into the office, taking off her jacket as she went down the hall. Grant stood at the desk. He turned slowly, hanging up the telephone.

She looked at him, and her heart turned to ice. His face—she'd never seen that expression on him before. Hard, implacable, determined. He looked at her as if he'd never seen her before. No, worse. As if she'd crawled out from under a rock.

"Hi." She forced a smile. "What's up?"

He gestured toward the phone. "That was Mrs. Hadley. You know her, right?"

Her heart wasn't frozen after all. Instead, it was beating so loudly she could hardly hear her own response. "I know Mrs. Hadley."

"You know her. And I know the truth. Finally." His words dropped like stones. "You're hiding the Bascom kids from social services."

Panic struck then. "You didn't say anything, did you? What did you tell her?"

"Nothing."

She pressed her hand against her chest. "Thank you."

"Don't thank me." He stalked toward her, face bleak. "I will tell her if I don't start hearing the truth from you right now. Why on earth are you hiding those kids? Are you trying to get the clinic shut down?"

"No, of course not." He couldn't think that. "I'm trying to help those children, that's all."

"By hiding them from the authorities? How is that helping?"

"The Bascom kids don't need social services. They

already have friends who'll take care of them until their mother gets back."

"Gets back from where?" Grant planted his fists on his hips and loomed over her, looking about ten feet tall. "Where is she, Maggie? How long has she been gone? Why does that Mrs. Hadley think she's run away?"

"I'm not responsible for what Mrs. Hadley thinks." If he'd stop hammering questions at her for a moment, maybe she could come up with an explanation he'd accept.

"Don't dance around it. Tell me the truth. What's going on?"

"All right!" She caught a breath. "It's not what you think. Nella isn't a bad mother."

"No? She's not here with her kids. What kind of mother does that make her?"

"She needed some time, that's all." She shook her head. "Maybe if you stopped shouting at me, I could explain things so you'd understand."

A muscle twitched in his jaw, but he nodded. "Fine. Explain."

*Please, Lord. Give me the words.*

"You already know the worst of it. Nella's husband abused her. We tried to help her, but she couldn't seem to break away. When he died, you'd expect her to feel free, but..."

She stopped, shaking her head. She tried to put herself in Nella's mind so she could understand. "I guess after living nine years with a man who dictated her every move, she couldn't think for herself any longer."

"You were trying to help her." There might have been a flicker of understanding in his eyes.

"I was trying to help her," she agreed. "We'd gotten her a job at the café, and Pastor Jim was counseling her. I thought she'd started to turn the corner. Then—"

"She left. Deserted her children." The implacable look was back.

"No, not deserted." She wouldn't believe that. "She left the kids at the clinic early one morning, with a note saying she needed to get her head together, but she'd be back for them. She's coming back."

He was shaking his head even while she spoke, the air between them sizzling with his disbelief. His disappointment in her. "She's gone, Maggie. She's left you holding the bag, and she's gone."

"She'll be back." Why couldn't he see what she was so sure of? "Look, you don't know Nella. She loves those children. She's called and written every few days. She'll come back."

"Wake up." Impatience laced his words. "Even if you're right about the woman, this isn't your responsibility. You shouldn't be taking care of them. Social services is equipped to do that. You're not."

Her temper flared. "I'm doing a good job with those children."

"That's not the point. Let the professionals handle the situation."

"That's what you'd do back in your city hospital, I suppose." She turned away, unable to keep looking at him through her hurt and disappointment. "Pick up the phone and turn them over to a stranger."

"If I didn't, I'd be breaking the law. Like you're doing right now."

She swung back to face him. "I'm not. I'm helping innocent children."

"You're breaking the law," he said implacably. "No matter how you rationalize it. And you're putting the clinic in jeopardy with your actions."

She wanted to deny that, but she couldn't. If the truth came out, it would give the county bureaucrats just the ammunition they needed to close the clinic. She'd known that all along, but she'd believed the children were worth the risk. She still did.

"Look, I'm sorry about deceiving you. But we—"

"We?" The single word cracked like a whip. "How many people know about this?"

She could only stare at him. "Why, everyone. Everyone in Button Gap. Except you, of course."

"Everyone?" Grant looked as if he'd been hit by a sledgehammer. Then his hand shot out to grab hers. "Think, Maggie. That means someone will tell. Someone probably already has told, or that social worker wouldn't have been asking questions."

"No one in town would do such a thing. Button Gap takes care of its own."

"Someone will talk." He let her go, rubbing his forehead as if the sight of her gave him a headache. "They'll close the clinic on my watch."

"Is that the only thing that's important to you? Your precious partnership?"

His mouth tightened. "The only chance is to come clean, right now." He gestured toward the phone. "You call, or I will."

"No!"

He wouldn't understand. He wouldn't take her word for it. Not unless she told him.

"Maggie—"

"No." She took a breath, tried to speak around the lump in her throat. "You don't see what's at stake. I do. I know what will happen to those children if they get caught up in the system before Nella returns."

"What are you talking about? How do you know?"

She couldn't. She had to.

"I know because I was like them. I know what I'm talking about because I *was* one of those kids."

"You were—"

She forced herself to meet his gaze. "My father abused my mother, abused me, until social services took me away. You'd say Mrs. Hadley was right. You'd say she did what was best for me."

He was processing the knowledge, coping with it, his eyes pained and serious. "She probably thought she did."

"Maybe so." She looked back into the darkness, trying not to flinch. "I just know that my life turned from one nightmare into another. It took me years to climb out. I won't let those children go through what I did. Not for you, not for anyone."

## Chapter Nine

Grant tried to absorb what Maggie was saying, but his heart hurt so much for her that it was hard to think straight. *Maggie.* All the pieces of her elusive personality started falling into place like so many toppling dominos.

He should have realized the truth before this—would have, if he hadn't been so preoccupied with his own concerns. He'd known she'd been sent to stay with Aunt Elly when she was just a child. He'd seen her fierce protectiveness toward the weak. Even her brief comments about her father were explained by this one significant fact.

He had to say something. "Maggie, I'm sorry. I didn't realize."

Some of the tension in her face eased slightly, as if she'd been prepared for a blow that she now knew wasn't coming.

"You couldn't have known. People here do, but no

one would tell an outsider, any more than they'd tell Mrs. Hadley about the Bascoms."

That was the crux of the situation. Even through his pain for Maggie, he knew he had to be cautious. He couldn't let his sympathy for her keep him from doing the right thing for those children.

"Maybe so."

He had to admit that she knew Button Gap far better than he ever could. He realized he was standing almost on top of her and eased back a step.

"Will you tell me about what happened to you? About why it makes you so sure you can't bring social services into this?"

Maggie wrapped her arms around herself in an attitude of protection, and for a moment he thought she'd refuse to answer him. Then he recognized that she was only arming herself to say the words.

"I was ten when the county sheriff came." Her eyes grew dark, distant, as if they were seeing that day once more. "My mother had given up trying to protect me by then. He could keep her home, but he had to send me to school, and the teacher saw the bruises."

His mind winced at the thought of bruises discoloring her skin, of the fear that must have lived in her eyes most of the time.

"Mrs. Hadley took me to a shelter. She wouldn't tell me where my mother was or what was going to happen to me. She didn't tell me anything, just left me there."

"You thought you were being punished."

She nodded. "I was. And I thought I deserved it."

Of course she had. Kids always seemed to blame themselves for the miserable things adults did.

"But you went to Aunt Elly eventually."

A ghost of a smile crossed her face. "Aunt Elly wouldn't give up. She kept badgering the county officials until they placed me with her."

"You were happy there."

"Happy?" She considered the question gravely. "Not for a long time. I guess I couldn't believe that she could love and protect me. Not when my own parents didn't."

He reached toward her, and then drew his hand back. She wouldn't welcome a touch at this moment.

"Eventually she got through to me. I started feeling like I belonged. Everyone here knew what had happened, and they were kind." Her lips tightened. "Then Mrs. Hadley took me away again."

"Why?"

She shrugged. "Who knows why that woman does anything? Because she could, I guess."

That didn't correspond to anything he'd experienced with social workers.

"I'm sure you've probably dealt with some wonderful caring people in children's services." Maggie seemed to be reading his thoughts. "But not here. Mrs. Hadley *is* that department, and she runs it like her own private kingdom. She bounced me from one home to another. Every time I started to feel safe, she'd move me again. The only thing I had to hold on to was the faith Aunt Elly had taught me."

If he let himself think too much about that lost child, he could never take action.

"You had a terrible time. But sometimes taking children away from parents is the only way to keep them safe. The Bascom kids—"

"The Bascoms *have* a good mother," she shot back. "My mother lost the will to protect me, if she'd ever had it. But not Nella. She never did. She always tried to protect her children."

How could he put this in a way that wouldn't hurt her? Maybe that was impossible.

"She ran away. You have to face that."

"She's just confused. Nella has a good heart. She'll do the right thing." Tears filled her eyes. "I can't let her return to find her family broken up. If those children are sucked into the system, she might never get them back. Even if she did eventually, they'd be...damaged."

*Like me.* He knew that was what she thought, and it grabbed his heart and wouldn't let go.

This wasn't just about Nella and her children. Maggie needed, at some very deep level, to believe that this would work out right for the Bascoms. This was for Maggie's sake, too, to heal that damaged place inside her.

Maybe she sensed that his conviction was weakening. She took a step toward him and put her hand on his arm.

"Please, Grant. Give this a chance. If you don't believe I'm right about the children, talk to them. Get to know them better before you do anything. You'll see that they belong with Nella."

Her grip compelled him to respond. He shook his head, trying to think rationally, but the pain Maggie carried around had fogged his vision.

"I don't know," he said finally. "I don't know if the system would work any better for the Bascom kids than it did for you."

"Then how can you say we should risk it?" The passion in her voice, in her eyes, shook him.

We. If he didn't call the Hadley woman back, right now, he was in this nearly as deeply as Maggie was.

The truth was that Maggie had put him between a rock and a hard place, and any decision he made could lead to the demise of the clinic and probably his partnership, as well. He moved a step away from her, as if that would make it easier.

It didn't. He still felt the pressure of her need to keep the children safe.

He sighed, knowing he couldn't take the easy way out, not now.

"No promises, Maggie. But I won't say anything without thinking it over first and telling you."

Joy flooded her face, but before she could say anything, he shook his head.

"This isn't approval. I still think what you're doing is too risky. But the clinic is already implicated, so I won't act without thinking it through."

Her eyes shone. "Thank you."

"Don't thank me." That probably came out harshly, but he couldn't seem to help it. "I don't know what I'm going to do."

He knew one thing, though. He was letting his sympathy for those kids and his pain for Maggie drag him close to disaster.

"Will you kids please stop stampeding through the living room?"

Three small faces swung toward her, and Maggie saw the apprehension in them. The children were bathed and dressed for bed, and they looked like three Christmas elves in their footed red pajamas.

"It's okay." She shouldn't have snapped at them. It wasn't the children's fault that she still held on to the residue of that confrontation with Grant, like bitter dregs in the bottom of a cup. "I just don't want galloping horses to knock over the Christmas tree, all right?"

Joey nodded solemnly. "We'll be careful."

"Good enough. I'm going to finish up the dishes, and then we'll have a story before bed."

"The Christmas story," Tacey said, and ran to the bookshelf to pull out the tattered Christmas storybook that Aunt Elly had given Maggie years ago.

"Okay. The Christmas story."

Maggie went back to the sink. The black cloud over her head lifted slightly with the memory of that Christmas when she'd begun to feel she belonged with Aunt Elly. She'd actually felt safe for the first time in her life.

She dried the glass milk pitcher carefully and put it in the cabinet. The ordinary routine soothed her, and she tried to look rationally at what had happened between her and Grant that morning.

He knew the truth now, in spite of all her efforts to prevent that. What would he do with it?

At least he'd promised not to do anything without talking to her again. He'd keep his word. She understood him well enough to be sure of that.

Beyond that, she tried to think past his knowing about Nella and the children. She couldn't. She couldn't wipe out the memory of his expression when he'd looked at her as if she were a stranger. She couldn't imagine what he was thinking or planning now.

One fact stood out with perfect clarity in the midst of a fog of uncertainty. Whatever friendship or relationship had been building between them had been shattered to bits. She'd never put it together again.

She gripped the edge of the sink until the pain subsided. She'd already known that a real relationship between them wasn't possible. So she had nothing to grieve over. You couldn't mourn something that had never been, could you?

All she cared about now was what he did about the children. She wouldn't let herself think of anything else. Grant meant nothing to her now but a potential threat to the children. Nothing at all.

A knock at the door set her heart hammering against her ribs. The kids, playing noisily in the living room, hadn't heard.

Was she going to panic every time someone knocked

on her door? Relive the nightmare of Mrs. Hadley coming to take her away?

She steeled herself and opened the door to find Grant standing on her porch.

Her throat tightened. He'd said he wouldn't expose them without telling her first. Was that what brought him?

"Grant." She gripped the doorknob, suppressing the longing to slam the door.

"May I come in?" When she didn't move, his eyebrows lifted. "You invited me to get to know the kids better, remember?"

She could breathe again. He hadn't come to deliver an ultimatum. She stepped back.

"Of course. Come in."

He stamped loose snow from his shoes onto the mat, then slid his jacket off. He'd changed from the dress shirt he wore in the office to a forest-green sweater that made his eyes look more green than blue.

"Is this a bad time?"

"No." She nodded toward the living room. "They're having a game before bedtime. Go on in."

She almost moved to join him, but then knew instinctively that she shouldn't. If Grant were to be convinced that those children belonged with Nella, the kids would have to do it, and without her help. Grant already felt that she couldn't be trusted.

A sliver of pain pierced her at the thought. She turned back to the sink, trying to hold it at bay.

*What can't be cured must be endured.* One of Aunt

Elly's homilies drifted through her mind. True enough. Sometimes a person just didn't have a choice.

She dawdled over the washing up, listening to the noises from the other room. By the sound of things, they'd pulled Grant into playing with the battered board game she'd gotten out for them.

They were all right. She was the one in need of emotional first aid.

*Lord, I need some help here.* She tried to think how to pray. *Grant knows, and somehow I've got to keep him on our side in all this. Please, show me how to do it. Open his heart to know what's right.*

Grant had a grudge against God. She didn't know how or why she knew that, but she was sure of it.

*Open his heart to You, Father. He doesn't seem to know that he needs healing, too. Amen.*

Slowly the tension drained out of her. Much as she'd like to think she could do everything herself, she couldn't. God was in control, and she had to believe He'd bring Grant around in His own time.

She moved to the doorway, watching the four of them clustered around the game board. The tip of Tacey's tongue protruded slightly as she clicked her plastic token along the path of the game.

"Five. I won!"

That was the loudest she'd ever heard Tacey speak. Grant's gaze met hers, and she could tell he was thinking the same thing.

He smiled at the little girl. "You won, all right. Good job."

Robby pouted. "I never win."

"Next time." Tacey leaned over to pat his shoulder. "Next time you'll probably win. You'll see."

"Can we play another game?" Joey snatched up his game token.

"Tomorrow." Maggie handed him the box. "Let's put it away for now. It's time for bed."

Did Grant realize what he was seeing? She worried at it as the children put the game away and tidied up the other toys.

Did he understand that children were only considerate and helpful if they had a mother who'd cared enough to instill that? The Bascom kids were a credit to Nella, who'd done a good job with them under the worst of circumstances.

The kids scampered up the narrow wooden stairs, followed by Maggie. To Maggie's surprise, Grant went up with her. She'd thought his interest wouldn't extend to more than a game, but apparently he intended to help put them to bed.

That was good, wasn't it? It had to mean he was trying to see things through their eyes.

All three of them slept in her small guest room— Joey and Tacey in the twin beds, Robby in the trundle bed. The eaves came down on both sides, making the room a cozy nest.

"It's better for Robby to be there," Tacey explained gravely to Grant, patting the trundle. "'Cause sometimes he falls out of bed, and this way it isn't too far."

"That's a good idea." Grant tucked the patchwork quilt around her.

Tacey handed him the Bible storybook. "Do you want to read the story tonight?"

He looked at the book for a moment, then passed it to Maggie. "We'll let Maggie read it tonight, okay? I'll just listen."

She opened the book, her mind scrambling to think of a story that might touch him. Then she glanced at the page. The book had fallen open to the story of the three kings.

Her mind flashed back to that night at the Christmas pageant rehearsal. Perhaps there was a connection between Grant and the rich men who'd brought their gifts.

*Open his heart, Lord,* she whispered silently.

She couldn't ask for a better audience than the three children to hear the old familiar story. They listened raptly, but Grant's eyes were shuttered, telling her nothing of what he felt.

When the kings had gone home again by another way, she closed the book and put it on the bedside table. "Let's say prayers, now. Who wants to start?"

Tacey folded small hands. "Now I lay me…" The two boys joined in.

"And please God bless Mommy and bring her home soon. Amen."

"Amen," Maggie added softly, and bent to kiss the child's soft cheek.

She moved toward the other bed, smiling as Joey

ducked away from her kiss. It was a game they played every night. Joey wanted the kiss, but his manhood demanded that he declare it mushy.

She bent over Robby, then realized that Tacey was holding out her arms to Grant. Maggie's heart twisted. She'd never seen Tacey voluntarily hug a man before. Did he even realize—

Then she saw the sheen of tears in Grant's eyes, and she knew he understood.

She stood, and Grant joined her in the doorway. "You get to sleep now, okay?"

On a chorus of agreement, she closed the door.

Grant didn't speak as they went down the stairs, but the silence wasn't uncomfortable. It was oddly intimate. They might be two parents, planning to spend a quiet evening together after the children were in bed.

She jerked her mind away from that dangerous thought. She couldn't go letting herself imagine anything of the kind. The best she could hope for from Grant was that he wouldn't turn them in.

He stopped in the middle of the living room. He might have been staring at the Christmas tree, but she had a feeling he didn't see it.

Finally he looked at her. "All right. You win."

Her breath caught. "What do you mean?"

"I understand why you feel the way you do about those kids and their mother. I just hope you're right about her. But whether you are or not, I won't turn you in."

"Thank you." She breathed the words, her eyes filling

with tears that she tried to blink away. "It's going to work out all right. You'll see."

"I wish I had your confidence." His mouth tightened. "Even with the best intentions in the world, we may not win. You realize that, don't you?"

"I know."

*Thank you, Lord.*

We, he'd said. In spite of everything, Grant was in this with her. She couldn't ask for more than that.

Grant dug the snow shovel into the layer of fresh snow on the front walk. The additional snowfall hadn't amounted to more than a couple of inches, but it seemed to have made people want to stay home. He and Maggie had cut afternoon clinic hours short when the waiting room stayed empty.

Strictly speaking, he didn't suppose it was his job to clear the clinic sidewalks, but if he didn't, the task would undoubtedly fall to Maggie. She certainly had enough to do.

For a moment he saw her the way she'd looked the previous evening, her dark eyes shimmering with tears and reflecting the lights from the Christmas tree. He'd wanted to kiss her.

Now where had that thought come from? He'd already decided that was one temptation he wouldn't give in to again. Maggie wasn't the kind of person who'd indulge in a frivolous affair, even if he were so inclined. Her life was wrapped up in her work, her people, her faith and those kids.

So he wasn't going to think about her that way. He'd concentrate on how good it felt to get in some physical activity. Button Gap didn't have a convenient health club, but that didn't mean he had to sit around.

He hefted another mound of snow with the battered old shovel he'd found in the back hall. Amazing how heavy the snow was despite the fact that it looked so light and fluffy. He was actually working up a sweat.

The door to Maggie's place slammed. Joey ran across the porch, used the snow shovel he carried as a vaulting pole and skidded to a stop next to him.

"Maggie says I can help you shovel," he said importantly. "The other kids are too small, but I can help."

"Sounds good."

He tried to think if he'd ever approached a chore with such enthusiasm when he was a kid. Probably not, but then, nobody had expected him to do anything but get high grades and be polite. Joey might be a little rough around the edges, but he had a good heart.

"You know what?" Joey shoveled energetically, sending snow flying. "I was thinking about that story Maggie read last night."

"The three wise men?" He hoped his comments about the number of wise men in the pageant weren't going to come back to haunt him.

"Yeah, those guys." Joey paused, shovel poised. "Seems like, if they were rich guys, maybe even kings, they should've given Baby Jesus something better."

He tried not to smile. "Better than gold?"

"What's a baby gonna do with gold?" Contempt filled Joey's voice.

"You might have a point there," he admitted.

"What's that frankincense stuff, anyway?"

Joey seemed filled with questions on a subject Grant would prefer to ignore.

"What makes you think I know?" he countered.

The boy's nose wrinkled. "Well, you gotta know stuff like that. I mean, you're a grown-up and a doctor. You oughta know everything."

"Everything is a tall order." He dredged through long-ago memories of Sunday school classes. "I think frankincense was something sort of like perfume. It had a sweet smell. And myrrh is a kind of spice."

"Well, there you go." Joey flung his hands out in disgust. "What would a baby want with stuff like that?"

Grant would have liked to tell the boy to go ask Maggie, but something insisted that Joey deserved an answer from the grown-up he'd asked.

"Those were considered presents fit for a king," he said. "That showed that the wise men understood who Jesus was." And he was certainly the last person in the world who ought to be explaining theology to an eight-year-old.

"Oh." Joey digested that. "You mean like he was God's son."

The kid had a grip of the essentials, anyway. "Yes."

"Well, I still think he'd have liked something else better. Like a red toboggan, maybe." Joey's eyes grew wistful. "A person could go awful fast on a red toboggan, with all this snow."

Baby Jesus hadn't needed a red toboggan, but he suspected he knew who did. "Maybe you'll get one for your birthday or for Christmas."

Joey shook his head and sent another shovelful of snow flying. "No. My mama can't afford something like that. It doesn't matter. I can get on fine without one."

For a moment he was speechless. The child's calm acceptance of what he couldn't have shamed him with reminders of all the expensive toys that had been piled beneath his Christmas tree over the years.

"You wanna know a secret?" Joey leaned close, as if someone might be lurking in the nearest snowdrift.

Grant nodded.

"I'm making something special for Maggie for Christmas. Aunt Elly's helping me. It's a really nice pot holder so she won't burn herself when she takes stuff out of the oven. You think she'll like it?"

He discovered there was a lump in his throat. "I think she'll love it."

"Hey, guys!" Maggie stood in the doorway. "How about warming up with some hot chocolate? It's all ready."

"You bet." Joey scrambled toward the house.

He probably shouldn't. Being around Maggie only seemed to make him do things he'd never expected, like hiding three kids from the authorities. To say nothing of feeling things he'd be better off not feeling.

But Maggie was holding the door open, and he found himself following Joey inside.

"You both did a great job on the walk."

Maggie settled the kids around the coffee table with their chocolate, then put a plate of cookies within reach. She tousled Joey's hair, and the boy grinned, then winked at Grant, apparently reminding him to keep his secret.

Maggie went into the kitchen, and he followed, using the sink to wash his hands.

"Would you rather have coffee than hot chocolate?" Maggie lifted the pot from the stove.

"No, the chocolate is fine." He dried his hands. "Smells good."

"You were looking very solemn. I thought maybe you didn't like hot chocolate."

"I was thinking about my conversation with Joey. He has a better understanding than a lot of adults about what it meant for Baby Jesus to be poor and alone."

"I suppose he does." There was a question in her eyes, but she didn't ask it.

"He's making gifts for Christmas." He shook his head. "I honestly think he's more excited about what he's giving than what he's getting."

Maggie considered that, head tilted to one side, her glossy dark hair swinging against her cheek. "That's the way it should be, isn't it?"

"I suppose so. It often isn't." He frowned, knowing he wasn't doing a very good job of putting his feelings into words. "He just made me realize that I've never given anyone a gift that really cost me."

Maggie probably thought he was crazy. He certainly sounded that way.

"Look, I'd like to get something special for Joey's birthday tomorrow. Where can I find a red toboggan?"

Her eyes widened. "Do you mean that?"

"I wouldn't say it if I didn't mean it." He moved impatiently, suddenly wanting to run out and do this. "I know you got a saucer for him, but—"

"That's all right. He'll share that with the little ones, and he'd adore a toboggan. But, Grant, they're awfully expensive."

He shrugged. Maggie's idea of awfully expensive probably wasn't the same as his.

"That doesn't matter. Where can I get it?"

"You'll have to drive down to Millerton. You came through it on your way here. There's a hardware store right on Main Street that would have them. But—"

"Good." He grabbed his jacket. "I'll go now, before they close."

"But it's so expensive," she repeated. Her eyes were troubled.

"Not for me," he said honestly. "That's what I meant when I said I'd never given a gift that cost me. I've never had to sacrifice anything to give to someone else." He caught her hands in his. "Let me do this, okay?"

"Okay." She lifted her face toward him with a smile.

He shouldn't. He was going to.

He drew her toward him and kissed her, feeling the

startled movement of her lips against his. Then he let her go and bolted out the door before he could give in to the desire to keep right on kissing her.

## Chapter Ten

Grant should be here soon. Maggie glanced at the clock as she forked fried chicken onto a platter. He wouldn't miss Joey's birthday, not after he'd driven down to Millerton the day before for that toboggan.

They'd promised Joey his favorite meal. Aunt Elly bustled to the stove, bearing a plate of sweet corn from her own garden that she'd frozen for winter. Sweet corn and fried chicken—that was all he'd wanted. The birthday cake and presents would probably send him into orbit.

A knock at the door sent Joey racing to it. He flung the door open, and his face fell. It was Grant.

"Hi, Joey." Grant stepped inside, giving Maggie a questioning look.

"Okay, you kids scoot into the other room so we can get this meal on without you underfoot." She shooed them. "It'll be ready in a couple of minutes."

As they stampeded into the living room, Grant turned from greeting Aunt Elly, his eyebrows lifting.

"I think he's been secretly hoping his mother would get here for his birthday," she explained. "That's why he looked disappointed."

Grant's mouth tightened. "She should be here."

"I know." She rubbed her arms, feeling chilled, as if the cold air had come in with Grant. Maybe she'd been secretly hoping that, too. But Nella hadn't come.

"Well, let's get this food on." Aunt Elly wiped her hands on her apron. "No sense fussing over what we can't do anything about."

"Right." Maggie pasted a smile on her face and went to get the chicken. All she could do at the moment was to make sure Joey had a good birthday. She'd worry about Nella later.

After a few minutes of the inevitable last-minute rush, they were all seated around the table.

"Joey, you're the birthday boy." Maggie reached out to him on one side and Grant on the other. "You say the blessing."

Joey, eyes wide at the sight of his favorite dishes, nodded and grabbed her hand. "God-bless-this-food-and-bless-us-Amen." He reached for the chicken.

She started to correct him, but Grant squeezed her hand just then, and she lost track of what she'd intended to say. By the time he'd let go and she could think rationally again, Joey had already passed the platter.

Grant picked up an ear of corn. "This actually looks fresh." He tasted. "How on earth did you get sweet corn at this time of year?"

Aunt Elly smiled, satisfied. "Picked fresh from my

garden in August. No more than ten minutes from the garden to my freezer."

"Sure is good." Robby seemed to be wearing butter from ear to ear. "I'm glad it's Joey's birthday."

"Me, too," Tacey said.

Joey dug into his food, and Maggie began to relax. Of course he was disappointed that Nella wasn't here, but it would still be a good birthday. He couldn't help but enjoy himself, especially when he saw the gift Grant had waiting on the porch outside.

They'd eaten their way through the whole platter of corn, most of the chicken and huge wedges of Aunt Elly's double chocolate cake, when someone knocked on the door. Again, Joey darted to answer, hope and caution warring in his expressive face.

"Are you Joseph Bascom?" The deliveryman held a paper-wrapped parcel.

Too awed to show disappointment that it wasn't Nella, Joey nodded.

"Then this is for you." The man handed it over, glanced toward the table and smiled. "Happy Birthday."

"Thank you." Joey shut the door and then turned to them, holding the package in both hands. "I got something. He said it's for me."

"So we see. Do you want some help opening it?" Grant said.

Joey shook his head. As if the question had jolted him out of his wonderment, he plopped down on the floor and ripped the box open.

"Cars!" He took out three small metal cars. "Look,

Robby. I got three cars, brand-new ones. And an airplane."

Tacey and Robby hovered over him, awestruck.

"Looks like there's a card," Maggie pointed out, praying it was from Nella.

Joey ripped it open, frowning as he deciphered the words. He looked up finally, and she could see he was fighting back tears. "It's from Mama. She's sorry she's not here. She loves us."

There was a lump in her throat the size of one of the eggs from Aunt Elly's geese. She swallowed. "Of course she does. You know, I think there might be some other presents around here, too."

She went to the pantry and carried out the snow saucer.

"A saucer!" Joey squealed.

Almost before she could put it down, all three children were sitting on it, momentary sorrow gone. Joey wore a grin from ear to ear.

Then it was Aunt Elly's turn to get out the gift she'd hidden when she came in. "Here's something to keep you warm when you play in the snow."

He ripped off the paper and shook out a hand-knitted red muffler. "Wow." He put the muffler around his neck and stroked it. "I never had a birthday like this before. Never."

"Seems as if there's something out here for you." Grant reached onto the porch and lifted in the red toboggan, holding it out to the boy.

If she lived to be a hundred, she didn't think she'd

see a better sight than Joey's expression at that moment. Awe, wonder and disbelief chased each other across his face.

"For me?" He reached out tentatively, as if not quite daring to touch it.

"For you." Grant put it in his hands.

"Wow." Joey seemed to have lost the ability to say anything else. "Wow."

Grant looked—

Maggie had trouble classifying that expression. Pleased, she supposed, that his gift was so well received. But almost ashamed, as well, as if it shouldn't be so easy to make someone so happy.

"What do you think?" Grant ruffled Joey's hair. "You want to take it out in the yard and give it a try?"

All three of the children rushed for their coats, and in a moment the adults were alone with the dirty dishes.

"Well, that boy won't soon forget this birthday." Aunt Elly started to clear the table. "But I reckon he'd give all the presents back if he could have Nella here."

"I know." Maggie picked up an empty platter. "I just wish—"

"If wishes were horses, beggars would ride," Aunt Elly said firmly. "This doesn't take wishing. It takes doing something about."

"I agree." Grant stood up, his palms braced on the table. "You saw Joey's face when he realized his mother wasn't going to come. We have to do something."

She pushed away the sense that they'd both turned against her. They wanted what was best for the children—she knew that. "I know." She rubbed at the ache that had begun in her temples. "I'd hoped and prayed Nella would come back on her own, but I've let it go on too long. I'll have to go after her."

Grant caught her arm, swinging her to face him. "What do you mean, go after her? Do you mean to say you've known all along where she is?"

"Not exactly." Her heart sank. As if everything else wasn't enough, she'd given Grant one more reason to distrust her. "I have an idea, that's all. About a place where Nella used to live. That's where her letters have been postmarked."

"I see." His face had tightened to an impenetrable mask. "You didn't bother telling me that."

She didn't have any response that would make a difference in what he thought.

"I'll go and find her. I'll leave first thing in the morning."

"Good." Grant's expression didn't change. It was still armored against her. "And I'm going with you."

Grant gripped the steering wheel as he waited for Maggie to come back out of the roadside café. They'd closed the clinic for the day and left early. The drive to West Virginia had been done mostly in silence. He hadn't known what to say to Maggie that wouldn't make him angry all over again that she hadn't told him.

The sight of Joey being so brave about his disappointment had ripped through his heart. It was as if being in Button Gap had stripped away his professional barriers, making him vulnerable to the child's pain in an intensely personal way.

He didn't like being vulnerable. Of course he had to care for his patients as a physician, but he'd always kept that solid, professional shield in place. It was the only way he knew to go on functioning.

Maggie came out of the café, juggling two foam coffee cups. He reached across to open the car door for her, and she handed him one.

"No luck," she said, sliding into her seat. "No one there has seen Nella."

He took a sip of the coffee, then consulted the map he'd put on the dashboard. "We'll be in Brampton in another half hour. It looks like a decent-size town. How do you propose we look for Nella?"

He could feel the caution in her gaze. This was the most he'd said to her in hours.

"I thought we'd start with the phone book. Nella's maiden name was Johnson—unfortunately pretty common, but maybe we'll hit some relatives."

"You're not thinking of just phoning them, are you? If she's hiding, it would be too easy for them to say they hadn't heard from her."

She shook her head. "No, I figure we'll have to go to every address we can find."

"And if that doesn't work?" He had to keep pushing, in case there was something else she hadn't told him.

"The only job Nella's ever had is waitressing. We'll just have to start working our way through the restaurants and cafés."

He started the car and pulled onto the highway. "That could take days." He didn't relish spending his time poking around a strange town, looking for a woman he'd never met. "Maybe we should have called in a private investigator. Or the authorities."

"No!" Her glare singed him. "You agreed to give me a chance to find her first. And if you think this is a waste of your time, you didn't have to come."

"Yes, I did have to come. I couldn't trust you to do this on your own."

The words hung in the air between them like an indictment, and he saw her wince. Well, that was how he felt. Maggie hadn't told him any more of the truth than she'd been forced to, and he'd swallowed every word.

She was silent for so long that he didn't think she'd respond. Then she set her cup carefully into the holder and clasped her hands in her lap.

"I'm sorry. I know I should have told you."

"Yes. You should have." He wasn't in a mood to make this easy for her.

"Why?" She fired the word at him. "You're saying I should have trusted you with Nella's whereabouts. Why? All you've been able to say since you found out about the kids is that I should turn them over to the authorities."

"That's not fair, Maggie. I agreed to wait, in spite of the danger to the clinic."

"That's another thing. I thought you preferred to know as little as possible. At least that way you're not implicated personally."

He clenched the steering wheel, because what he'd

like to do was grab Maggie and shake her. "I became involved the minute the clinic did. You know that."

He glanced at her. She was leaning forward, staring out the windshield, as if willing the car to go faster.

"All right, the clinic is involved," she said finally. "But you're asking why I didn't trust you." Her hands gripped each other tightly. "Rely on you. And I guess the answer is that I don't rely on people easily."

"You trusted the rest of Button Gap. Everyone in town knew but me."

"I've known them most of my life. I've only known you a few weeks, and even if—" She stopped, turning her face away from him.

How had she intended to finish that sentence? Even if you kissed me? Even if I cared for you?

He pulled away from that line of thought. It couldn't go anywhere.

"Look, I know how much you care about those kids. I understand why you don't trust the system. But they're not the only ones involved. How will everyone else in Button Gap get along if the clinic closes?"

"That's not fair. Everyone agreed to help."

"Sure they did. But you and I are the professionals. We're the ones who know the rules. If someone gets blamed for this, it will be us. And the clinic." They'd traveled full circle, and it didn't seem they were any closer.

"We won't let that happen." She turned toward him. "For everyone's sake, we have to find Nella. And we will find her."

"I hope you're right, Maggie." He glanced in the rearview mirror to change lanes. "Because here's the exit, and I've got to say I don't feel all that confident."

A few hours later, Maggie's confidence had begun to fade. She tried to pump it up, but it was useless. They were down to the last Johnson in the phone book, and the afternoon was wearing on. If this one didn't know anything, it would be time to start checking on restaurants, and that hope seemed more futile as the hours passed.

Maybe Grant had been right. She glanced at him as he pulled to the curb in front of the cottage listed to a Mrs. Helen Johnson. A private investigator would have done this better, but she didn't have the money to pay one.

Grant did. He hadn't offered, and she wouldn't ask.

He got out. "Are you coming?"

"Of course." She tried to put some energy into her steps as she got out and started up the walk. Grant had been doubtful all along. She couldn't let him guess that she didn't feel so sure of success, either.

She knocked on the door, taking a quick look around. The cottage seemed to sag into itself, as if it had given up a long time ago. She knocked again, and the graying lace curtain on the window twitched.

"Mrs. Johnson?" she called. "Can you come to the door, please?"

She heard shuffling footsteps from inside that moved slowly toward the door. Next to her, Grant shifted his weight from one foot to the other. Impatient.

The door creaked open a few inches, displaying a safety chain and beyond it, a small, wrinkled face topped by scanty white hair.

"What do you want? If you're collecting for something, I can't afford to give."

"We're not collecting for anything, Mrs. Johnson." She tried a reassuring smile. "We're looking for someone we thought you might know. Nella Johnson Bascom."

"Don't know her."

The door started to swing shut, but Maggie got her foot into the space, something in the woman's tone triggering a nerve.

"Think hard, Mrs. Johnson. Isn't Nella a relative of yours?"

Caution flickered in the woman's faded eyes. "Never heard of her."

She knew something. Maggie wasn't sure how she knew, but she did. "Come on, now. I know she came to see you."

"I don't know nothing, I tell you." The querulous voice rose. "Now get away before I call the police."

"Maggie—"

She could tell by Grant's tone that he was picturing them ending the day in jail. He took her arm.

"Just another minute." She leaned close to the door. "Please, Mrs. Johnson. If you won't talk to us, talk to Nella. Tell her that Maggie was here. Tell her that her kids need her. Tell her to come home."

The woman blinked slowly, as if taking it all in, and then shook her head. "I told you. I don't know her."

"Come on." Grant tugged at her arm. "You might want to get arrested, but I don't."

Reluctantly she took her foot from the door. "Please. Tell her."

The door slammed shut.

Maggie bit her lip. "She knew something. I could tell. Couldn't you?"

Grant shrugged as he piloted her off the porch. "Maybe. But you can't force her to talk." He led her down the walk and opened the car door, frowned as if about to say something she wouldn't like, and then shrugged. "Let's go try some restaurants."

Over the next few hours they worked their way up one side of the town's small business district and down the other. Maggie's optimism flagged along with her energy. *Nella, where are you?*

Grant pulled into the parking lot of yet another restaurant.

"This looks like a decent place." He held the door for her. "Let's order dinner while we make inquiries. I think we need to regroup."

The restaurant's interior was warm and candlelit after the chilly dampness outside. Maggie slipped her coat off as Grant consulted with the hostess and showed her the photo of Nella. The woman shook her head.

Grant hung her coat and his on the wall rack as the hostess picked up menus.

"Nothing?"

"She didn't recognize her." Grant touched her arm,

maybe in sympathy, as they followed the hostess to a table.

Maggie wilted into the padded chair. "I don't know what else to suggest. I've wasted our time."

"Not necessarily. Maybe you were right about that Johnson woman. She might give Nella your message."

"And I might have been totally off base." She leaned her forehead on her hand.

"You'll feel better when you've had something to eat." He handed her a menu. "Pick something, or I'll do it for you."

"I thought you were only bossy in the clinic." She scanned the menu.

"No, that's my natural state." He smiled, as if he'd somehow gained the confidence she'd lost. "We're not licked yet."

She started to say she wished she could be so sure, but the waitress came to take their order and the moment was gone.

Grant steered the conversation to non-Nella topics while they ate, as if determined to have their meal without arguing. It was only when they lingered over coffee that he gave her a long, serious look.

"You're losing hope, aren't you?"

A lump formed in her throat. "I don't want to. I still hope Nella will come back. She said so in her note. Doesn't that show that she intends to return?"

Maybe it was the flickering candlelight that softened his firm features. He almost looked sorry for her.

"I don't know. You forget, I don't know Nella."

"You know her children. They're a reflection of her. Everything good in them came from Nella. It surely didn't come from that worthless husband of hers."

"They're good kids." He hesitated, making small circles on the white tablecloth with his coffee spoon. "But you have to remember that Nella spent a lot of years in a terrible situation. Maybe she just doesn't have it in her to keep on struggling."

"I don't believe that. I can't." She thought of her mother, and tension gripped her throat.

He dropped the spoon and put his hand over hers, warming her. "I know. Believe me, I hope you're right about Nella. But how much longer can we hope to hide those children from the authorities?"

"We can't give up yet." She wasn't sure anymore whether she was hanging on by conviction or plain stubbornness. "We can't."

"A little while ago you looked ready to."

"As you said, I needed to eat. And I guess, in the back of my mind, I always felt sure I could find Nella if I had to. Not finding her today rocked me."

She pulled out the picture of Nella with the children and put it on the table, as if it might speak to her.

"I can't give up," she said firmly. "Those kids deserve someone who believes."

The server came back with Grant's credit card receipt, and he absently put out his hand for it. "It was a good guess that Nella might be here. We just—"

The woman leaned over, staring at the photo. "Hey,

that's Nella Bascom and her kids. Are you folks friends of hers?"

Maggie caught the woman's hand. "You know Nella?"

The server looked taken aback at the intensity in Maggie's voice. "Why? She in some kind of trouble?"

"No trouble," Grant said quickly. "We're friends of hers. I asked the hostess about Nella, but she didn't recognize her."

The waitress sniffed. "'Course not. Lisa, she only works a couple evenings a week. Nella's on days."

"We've been trying to reach her, but I lost her phone number." Maggie tried to keep the tension out of her tone. "Do you happen to know where she is?"

She held her breath while the woman looked her over, then Grant.

"Well, I'd like to help you," she said finally. "Thing is, Nella's not here anymore."

"Not here?" The words seemed to strangle her.

The waitress shook her head. "Manager said she called in yesterday. Said she wouldn't be able to work anymore. Said she was leaving town."

Maggie sank back in the chair, vaguely hearing Grant ask another question or two. No, the woman didn't know where Nella had gone. She'd just left, that's all.

She'd left. Maggie tried to believe that meant Nella was on her way home, but somehow she couldn't. Nella had gone. There was no place else to look. She'd failed.

## Chapter Eleven

Grant just sat for a moment, trying to decipher the expression on Maggie's face. In spite of her brave words, she looked nearer to defeat than he'd ever seen her.

He ought to be relieved, in a way. Their quest for Nella had failed, and Maggie would have to admit that there was nothing left to do but turn the whole situation over to the authorities and try to salvage what remained of the clinic's reputation.

He wasn't relieved. Frustrated, upset—but not relieved. How could he be, when the children's future hung in the balance along with that of the clinic?

He scribbled his name on the credit card receipt and vented his frustration by shoving his chair back. "Let's go. We can't do anything else here."

Maggie didn't move. Maybe she was numb, but in an odd way it made him angry. He'd rather Maggie fought him than sit there looking lost.

She let him help her on with her coat, let him take her arm as they went to the car. She got in, and he slammed the door with a little unnecessary emphasis. He felt her gaze on him as he got behind the wheel and turned the key.

He didn't attempt to pull out. He frowned at the heater, which was making a brave effort to put forth something besides cold air, then transferred the frown to Maggie. She was huddled in her coat, hands tucked into her pockets.

"I don't suppose there's any chance Nella's on her way home."

Maggie's shoulders moved slightly. "I'd like to think that. But if she left yesterday, where is she?"

He discovered he was looking for something hopeful to say, as if he and Maggie had traded places. "If she took the bus, she wouldn't make the time that we did driving."

"Even so, she'd surely have gotten there by now." Maggie massaged her temples. "And if she had, Aunt Elly would have called. She has my cell phone number."

He bounced his fist against the steering wheel. It didn't help. "We've wasted the day, then."

"You didn't have to come along." A little of Maggie's spirit flamed up. "I didn't ask you to."

"That's not the point." He knew perfectly well he'd volunteered to come. He wasn't sure he wanted to admit his motives for that, even to himself. "The point is, we're both involved in breaking the rules now, and we haven't gained a thing."

"Sometimes you have to break the rules."

"It doesn't pay." Didn't she see that? "You bent every

rule there is, and we're no further ahead. You could lose your job. Don't you understand that?"

She looked at him then, her mouth twisting a little. "I understand. It's already happened to me."

"What are you talking about?"

"My first job after I graduated." Her eyes looked very dark. "A man brought his wife into the emergency room. He said she'd fallen down the stairs. She hadn't."

"Did the woman tell you the truth?"

"At first she did. I reported it, of course. But before the cops arrived, the husband came back with flowers, told her how much he loved her, how sorry he was."

It was a familiar story to anyone who'd worked in an E.R. He knew how it ended. "She backed down and refused to prosecute."

Maggie's hands clenched together. "She was ready to go home with him. It would have been the same thing all over again, and next time she might die."

"I know." He put his hand over hers. They were cold, gripping each other. "But you did the right thing. If she wanted to leave—"

"I didn't let her." She looked at him defiantly. "I said her X-rays had shown a problem and talked an intern into ordering more tests. By the time it was caught, the police had arrived. Once we could tell her that he was locked up, they were able to get the truth."

He looked at her steadily. "And what happened to you?" He knew the answer to that one, too.

"I lost my job." Her lips trembled momentarily, and she pressed them together. "It was worth it."

"Maggie—" What could he do with someone like her? "You know as well as I do that she probably turned around and went right back to him as soon as she was out of the hospital."

"At least I gave her a chance."

"You sacrificed your job. Now you're probably going to pay the same price again. Don't you see that—"

He stopped. She wasn't answering. She couldn't.

Maggie—determined, stubborn, always strong Maggie—was crying. Tears spilled down her cheeks without a sound, and she made no effort to wipe them away.

"Maggie."

Softer this time. Then he put his arm around her and drew her against him so that her tears soaked into his shoulder.

"It's okay." He patted her gently, as he'd seen her pat the kids. "You've done everything you could."

She let out a shuddering breath that moved across his cheek. "I failed."

"You didn't. You did your best." He tried to think of something else encouraging to say, but he couldn't. Maggie was crying in his arms, and he couldn't find a way to comfort her.

Because the truth was that she probably had failed. Nella probably wouldn't come back. The children would end up in foster care.

And Maggie? He stroked her back, feeling the sobs that shook her.

Maggie needed so much to be the rescuer instead of

the victim that she could lose her way entirely if she
didn't save Nella and the children. And there didn't seem
to be one thing he could do about it.

Even if the organist hadn't been playing "Adeste
Fideles," Maggie would have known it was the Sunday
before Christmas. It was in the air—the scent of the
pine boughs on the chancel rail, the scarlet of poinsettias
banked in front of the pulpit, the rustle of anticipation.
She might be the only person in the sanctuary who
wasn't consumed with excitement over the approach
of Christmas.

All she could feel was dread as she glanced at the
three children sitting in the pew with her. How long?
How long until social services snatched them away?

She'd put Joey on her right, experience having taught
her it was best to sit between him and Robby if she was
to have a semblance of control during the service. Joey
was on the end, taking advantage of this position to
crane around and gape at each person who came into
the sanctuary during the prelude.

She touched his shoulder, turning him toward the
front, and he grinned at her, eyes sparkling. Her heart
clenched.

*Don't let me fail these children, Lord. Please, don't
let me fail.*

But how could she expect God to pull her out of this
situation? She was the one who'd gotten into it, so sure
she was right and that Nella would come back on her

own. She'd betrayed the secret to Grant. And she'd been so weak as to break down in front of him.

She should never have let that happen. Excuses came readily to her mind—she'd been exhausted, stressed, worried about Nella. But she couldn't lie to herself, and certainly not in the Lord's house.

She'd grown to care too much for Grant. She'd never intended to, and she hadn't even seen it coming. She'd been blindsided by the emotion. When had her initial dislike changed to grudging respect, and respect to liking? And liking to love?

*Love.* She forced herself to look unflinchingly at the word. She'd fallen in love with him.

Nothing could possibly come of it, even without the complication of the Bascom kids. They were far too different for that. But she loved him.

Worse, she'd shown him everything there was to know about her. He could use it against her.

But he hadn't.

All the way home from West Virginia on Friday night she'd waited for that, and it hadn't come. During office hours the day before, she'd been keyed up every moment for him to confront her about Nella and the children. He hadn't.

Instead, he'd been considerate. Kind. Almost as if he felt sorry for her.

Robby wiggled next to her, and she put her arm around him. He snuggled close, resting his head against her side, and her heart hurt again.

Grant probably did feel sorry for her. He'd *be* sorry,

too. But she suspected that wouldn't stop him from calling social services first thing Monday morning.

The prelude ended, and the organist played the first notes of "Joy to the World," the opening hymn. As she opened the hymnal, Joey leaned perilously far out into the aisle.

She grabbed him, glancing back to see what so attracted him, and her breath caught.

Grant. Grant had come to church for the first time since that night at the Christmas pageant rehearsal.

Before she could think what that might mean, he'd started down the aisle. As he passed them, Joey reached out to grab his arm.

"Sit with us, Doc." What Joey thought of as a whisper was loud enough to be heard all the way across the sanctuary. "We have room."

Grant sent her a questioning look, as if asking permission.

Everyone was watching them. She could hardly deny him a seat. She managed a smile and slid Tacey and Robby over to make room. He sat down, Joey between them on the worn wooden pew.

This shouldn't be worse than being alone with him at the clinic. After all, he could hardly bring up any painful subjects while they were worshiping.

Still, she fumbled for the hymnal page, her fingers suddenly clumsy. She was just thrown by the unexpectedness of it, that was all. What had led him into the service this morning?

"'Joy to the world, the Lord is come.'"

Voices sang out. Grant grasped the edge of her hymnal, holding it between them, and her vision blurred. What was he doing here?

The hymn ended on its triumphant, ringing note, and a rustle went through the sanctuary as the congregation sat down. She fixed her gaze firmly on Pastor Jim.

She would not look at Grant. She would not wonder why he was here, or what he was thinking. But she couldn't help being aware of his every breath, no matter how she tried.

She managed to keep her eyes fixed to the front until the Old Testament reading. Pastor Jim had chosen the passage from Isaiah.

"'For unto us a child is born, unto us a son is given.'"

Powerful emotion swept her at the words. That linking of the most intimate, personal love of a parent for a newborn child with the advent of the Lord of all creation—how could anyone not be moved by that?

Something, some infinitesimal tension emanating from Grant, pulled her attention irresistibly. She turned, just a little, so that she could see him.

He was struggling. Probably no one else in that sanctuary could guess at the emotions surging under his calm exterior, but she knew. It was as if they were connected at the most basic level.

Something was wrong between Grant and the Lord. She'd known that since the night of the pageant rehearsal. She didn't know what, and she didn't know how, but that inner warfare was coming to a head.

*Please, Lord.* She didn't know how to pray for Grant,

but she had to. *I hold Grant up to You, Father. You know the secrets of his soul. Touch him. Heal him.*

Through a jumble of emotions she tried to listen to the rest of the sermon. Her mind seemed able to pay attention at one level while all the time, underneath, a constant stream of prayer went on. *Touch him, Lord. Please.*

The service flowed on to its close. Pastor Jim raised his hands in the benediction, then paused, holding the congregation with his smile.

"And whatever you do, don't forget to be here tomorrow night for the pageant. It wouldn't be Christmas Eve without each and every one of you."

She rose automatically, shepherding the children into the aisle. Grant let them pass and then moved close behind her. She felt his hand on her back, guiding her toward the door. His touch sent a tremor through her. Longing, need, apprehension, all jumbled up together, leaving her knees weak.

She managed to smile and speak as she walked up the aisle, hoping she looked normal enough to everyone else. Pastor Jim shook hands with each of the children. As they scrambled down the steps, he took Maggie's hand in both of his.

"Everything okay?"

Apparently she wasn't looking normal, at least not to someone as observant as Pastor Jim.

"I'm fine."

He pressed her hand. "If you need me, you know I'm here for you."

"I know," she said softly.

She stepped through the doorway. A damp wind swept down the street, bringing a promise of snow. She shivered, pulling her coat around her.

Behind her, she heard the pastor greeting Grant, sounding as relaxed and friendly as if Grant attended every Sunday. If Grant felt embarrassed, his response didn't betray it.

"You're coming to the pageant tomorrow night, aren't you?" Pastor Jim was at his most persuasive. "Maggie and the children have worked so hard on it."

"I'll try," Grant answered evasively.

She started down the steps. Joey had found a patch of snow left on the church lawn and was busy packing a snowball.

"Joey." Her voice contained a warning.

The boy looked at her, grinned and dropped the handful of snow.

"We'd better get on home and fix some lunch," she began, then stopped when Grant touched her arm.

She glanced up and found her gaze trapped by his.

"Do you have a minute?" His voice was firm and determined, as if he'd made a decision and intended to carry it out, no matter what.

Something chilled inside her. "Not really. I was about to fix lunch for the children."

He frowned. "Can't Aunt Elly watch them for a while?"

"I don't—"

"I'll be glad to take care of them." Aunt Elly,

unfortunately, had heard. "Joey, Robby, Tacey, come on with me. You can play outside after you have lunch and change your clothes."

Before she could think of another excuse, Aunt Elly had tramped off, chasing the children in front of her.

She straightened her shoulders and managed to look Grant in the eyes. "What is it?"

"Let's take a walk." His face was grim. "I have something to tell you."

Her heart seemed to stop. Only one thing Grant might have to say would put that look in his eyes.

Grant could see Maggie's fear in the way she braced herself, as if preparing for a blow she knew would fall. That reminder of the abuse she'd suffered from her father dented his confidence, and for an instant he questioned himself.

He was doing the right thing—no, the only thing possible. In these circumstances, with the children's happiness at stake as well as the future of the clinic, he couldn't see any good solutions.

He could only do what his training had taught him to do. He had confidence in that, at least.

That didn't make it any easier to take a step that would cause Maggie pain. His heart clenched again. She'd endured so much already.

They'd covered most of Main Street without speaking. Still without saying anything, they turned as if in silent agreement onto the lane that wound toward the woods.

They'd come this way before, with the children, in search of that lopsided Christmas tree.

Last week's snow had gone from the roads, but it still lay in patches in the fields and the woods. Maggie tilted her head to look at the leaden sky.

"You'd better warm up your shovel. It's going to snow again."

He followed her gaze. The clouds didn't look any worse than usual to him. "How do you know?"

"I just know." Her lips twitched in what might have been an attempt to smile.

"Button Gap will have a white Christmas, then."

Two days until Christmas. Would he still be here? He'd been going over the question in his mind. Technically, his stint at the clinic lasted until the end of the week, but the volunteer doctor coordinator had given him the option of leaving to spend Christmas with his family.

Not that he had any intention of doing that. Christmas in the Hardesty mansion wasn't something that would warm the cockles of anyone's heart.

Still, he could leave. No one would blame him. He didn't have to let anyone know he was back in the city until the holiday had safely passed.

"I realized I never thanked you for going to West Virginia with me."

Maggie's voice sounded oddly formal, as if she had practiced saying that. Or maybe she was just trying to distract him from what she must know he intended to say.

"It was no problem."

The ironic thing was that he didn't need any distracting—he was distracted enough already. The thing he had to say kept tying his tongue in knots.

No. That wasn't what tripped him up. Each time he looked at Maggie, he found himself thinking instead how incredibly dear to him she'd become in such a short time. He wanted to stop dead in the road, pull her into his arms and kiss away the tension and fear in her dark eyes. He wanted to hold her close and feel her hair like silk against his cheek.

He wouldn't. But he wanted to.

All right, he had feelings for Maggie. Their footsteps scuffed along the gravel lane in perfect tempo, as if they'd been made to walk side by side.

But a relationship between them would never work. It was not just that they were too different. Lovers could surmount that difficulty.

They wanted different things out of life. That was what it came down to, and that was why they'd only hurt each other if they tried to build a relationship.

If everything about the Bascom children came out, if the clinic were closed on his watch, he might lose the partnership with Dr. Rawlins. He faced that. He'd deal with it. That wouldn't change the kind of life he wanted, nor the kind of life Maggie needed.

*Say it. Tell her.*

"Maggie—"

"I was surprised to see you in church today." She

rushed into speech as if to stop him. "You don't usually come."

"No."

He couldn't explain to Maggie what he led him into the sanctuary that morning. No, not led. Drove. Something drove him there, in spite of every intention to the contrary. He couldn't explain, because he didn't know himself.

He only knew that a battle was going on inside him, as if some part of himself that he'd buried a long time ago had risen up and demanded attention. He realized Maggie was waiting for more of an answer than his curt negative.

"I thought I'd like to hear Jim's Christmas sermon, that's all. He's a nice guy."

"He is. Does that mean you're leaving before Christmas?"

"No." Sometime in the last few minutes that seemed to have been decided for him. He wouldn't be a coward. He'd stay and face the consequences of what he had to do. "I owe the clinic the rest of the week. I'll work out my days."

*Tell her. Just say it.*

He stopped abruptly, catching her hand and turning her to face him. He didn't want to look at her, but he owed her that much, at least. He'd have to watch the fear in her eyes change to hate.

He pushed the words out. "I'll let the kids have Christmas with you. The day after, you have to call social services. If you don't, I will."

# Chapter Twelve

She was losing.

Maggie leaned against the kitchen sink, staring out the window through the steam created by her breath. Snow. As she had predicted, snow was falling. It was December the twenty-fourth, and they would have snow for Christmas.

And the next day, Nella's children would be scooped up by social services. She might never see them again.

She frowned at the bird feeder on the hemlock branch. A scarlet cardinal shared seed peacefully with three chickadees and a pair of nuthatches, until a blue jay swooped in, scattering the other birds.

She'd have to send Joey out with more seed. He loved that job.

Soon Aunt Elly would come tramping cheerfully through the snow to watch the children while she went to the clinic. It might have been any ordinary day. It would be, if she didn't know what was going to happen as soon as Christmas was past. The knowledge hung on her, weighing her down until it was an effort to move.

She should have known that this would be the end of it, from the moment Grant found out the truth about the kids. She'd thought her heart couldn't hurt any more, but thinking about Grant brought a fresh spasm of pain.

*Father, help me deal with this. Please, help me see the way.*

She tried to cling to the hope that some miracle would take place, bringing Nella home for Christmas. Hope seemed to be in short supply right now.

*Please, Father, give me a sign. Give me something to assure me that Nella will come back.* She rubbed her forehead, reminded of too many Biblical characters who'd asked God for a sign because they lacked in faith. *I believe, Lord. I just don't know what to do—about the children, about Nella, about Grant. Show me.*

She stood still for a moment, trying to listen, and then pushed herself away from the sink. If an answer were forthcoming, it hadn't jumped into her mind yet. Maybe she'd best get on with her work, and trust God to deliver His answer in His time.

The children were awfully quiet. That couldn't be good. With a vague sense of foreboding, she walked into the living room.

The kids weren't there. But her mother's glass angel lay shattered on the floor beneath the Christmas tree.

She knelt, reaching carefully for the pieces. Maybe she could—

No, she couldn't. No one could put this back together again.

A tidal wave of grief threatened to drown her, and she choked back a sob. Her last tangible tie to her mother was gone.

*What if God is showing you that the same is true for those children? You did ask for a sign, didn't you?*

She stood quickly, shaking off the fragments of glass as she shook off the treacherous thought. No, she wouldn't let herself believe that.

"Joey, Tacey, Robby, where are you?" She raised her voice. They had to be upstairs.

A small, scraping noise from the floor above said she was right.

"Come on down here. I just want to talk to you." Surely they knew by this time that she didn't talk with her fists, the way their father had done.

Another small sound, and then came reluctant footsteps. Tacey and Robby crept down the stairs. They halted at the far edge of the braided rug, not looking at her.

"Where's Joey?"

No answer.

She crossed to them and knelt. "Come on, guys, I'm not mad. I just want to know what happened to my angel. Did Joey knock it off the tree?"

Tacey gave an almost imperceptible nod. "He didn't mean to," she whispered.

"Sweetie, I know that. Where is he?" She glanced up

the stairs. "Joey? Come on down, okay? I'm not mad at you."

Nothing.

She trotted up the steps, apprehension knotting her stomach. It took two minutes to search the small upstairs. Joey wasn't there.

She hurried back down, her imagination racing ahead of her. "Tacey, you need to tell me. Where is Joey?"

The child didn't answer, but she looked toward the rack where Joey's jacket should have hung. It wasn't there, and his boots were missing.

She grabbed her own jacket, then swung to look at the other two. "You stay here, all right? I'm going to get Dr. Grant to stay with you."

They nodded, eyes wide.

She yanked the door open. The toboggan was gone from the porch. She hurried down to the yard. Joey must have left while she was upstairs dressing. She could make out small tracks, almost obliterated already by the steadily falling snow.

"Joey!" She took a breath of cold, wet air. "Joey! Answer me!"

The back door of Grant's apartment swung open. He held it wide with one arm. "What's wrong? Why are you shouting for the boy?"

She ran toward him, heart pounding. "Is Joey with you? Have you seen him?"

Grant stepped onto the porch, shaking his head. "Not this morning. Why all the fuss? He probably just came out to play in the snow."

"Then where is he?" She spread her hands toward the empty yard. "He knows he's not to go out of the yard without permission."

Grant lifted an eyebrow. "Aren't you overreacting a bit? He was probably excited about the snow and wanted to try out his toboggan. It wouldn't be the first time he forgot to ask permission for something."

"This time is different." Her sense of foreboding intensified. "He apparently knocked my angel off the tree and broke it. Maybe he was scared. He slipped out of the house while I was upstairs."

That superior look was replaced by something that might have been concern. "I'm sorry about your angel. I know how much it meant to you. But still, he might just be hiding around the house."

"You always like the easy answer, don't you?" That probably wasn't fair, but it was what she felt. She swung around, torn by the pull to run in several different directions at once. "I better see what I can get out of the other two."

She couldn't ignore Grant's quick footsteps behind her as she hurried back into the house. Heedless of the snow she tracked in, she bent down, hands on knees.

"Tacey, I need to know where Joey went. Come on, now. You have to tell me."

Tacey's lips trembled, and she pressed them together, shaking her head.

She felt Grant's hand on her shoulder, and for a fraction of a second she wanted to lean into that strong hand.

No. She couldn't. Grant had already shown he wasn't on her side. She had to do this herself.

Then Grant knelt next to her. He reached out to draw Tacey into the circle of his arms.

"Tacey, honey, you have to tell us where Joey is. I know you probably promised him you wouldn't say, but it's snowing hard outside, and he could get lost. It's not wrong to break a promise if it means helping someone else."

His voice was soft, gentle, wringing Maggie's heart. "You know, don't you?"

Tacey nodded slowly. "He was afraid. He didn't mean to break the angel."

"Sweetie, I know. I'm not mad." Maggie brushed a strand of hair back from the child's forehead. "Just tell us where he went."

Tacey sniffled, then rubbed tears away with the back of her hand. "He thought you'd be mad. He took his toboggan. He said he was going to find Mommy, and he wouldn't come back until he did."

The words hit her like a blow. Maggie pressed her hand to her chest, as if that might ease the pain. Joey, out in the snow somewhere, searching for his mother.

She scrambled to her feet and ran to the phone.

"What are you doing?"

Grant was up, too, striding across the room to her.

"Calling Aunt Elly to stay with the kids." She punched in the numbers. "I have to go look for him."

"You can't do that alone."

"No." Fresh pain swept her heart. This was one thing she couldn't do alone. "I'll get help."

"I'm going, too." His tone was uncompromising.

"Fine." She wouldn't take the time to argue. She hung up. "Aunt Elly doesn't answer, so she must be on her way. If you want to help, stay here until she comes. Then put on your warmest clothes and come to the church. We'll organize the search from there."

She didn't give him time to answer, just grabbed her cell phone and heavy boots and ran for the door.

Help. She had to have help. The thoughts kept time to her running feet. *Please, Lord. Please.*

Grant was right. This was one thing she couldn't do alone.

He'd never have believed a bunch of volunteers could organize so fast. Grant stood at the back of the sanctuary, watching as the fire chief assigned duties. Judging by his clothing, the man was a barber when he wasn't setting up a rescue, but he seemed cool and in control.

They weren't just fast, they were efficient. They might be volunteers, but they operated as smoothly as any professional unit he'd ever seen.

The sanctuary was crowded with people, summoned by the church bell that had stopped pealing only moments ago. But it didn't matter how full the room was. His gaze was pulled to Maggie, only Maggie.

She stood at the front, close by the communion table on which they'd spread a large-scale map of the township. Her face was tense, her body rigid. She was hurting, but she wouldn't give in to it. Not Maggie. She'd never give in.

The chief went rapidly through the grid, assigning areas. Those with snowmobiles would search the woods. Others would take the streets and roads.

Grant thought of the miles of forests on the mountains, and his fists clenched. If the boy had gone that way, what chance did they actually have of finding him, especially in this snowstorm?

Pastor Jim stepped forward. By the look of his clothes, he intended to be one of the rescue party, but he clearly had something to say in his pastoral role first. He raised his hands, and the sanctuary grew quiet.

"Friends, let's pause for a word of prayer."

Heads bowed throughout the room.

"Eternal Father, we know that You see everything. You know where Joey Bascom is right now. We ask that You be with him, keeping him safe, and with us, leading us to him. Amen."

Amens chorused through the sanctuary, and people moved quickly toward the doors, lining up in twos and threes. As they went out, several older women bustled in, carrying tureens and coffee urns. Clearly everyone in Button Gap had a role when things went wrong.

Grant fell into step with Maggie as she hurried toward the door. She shot him a quick, questioning look.

"You have an idea which way he's headed, don't you?"

She shrugged, trotting down the steps toward her truck. He kept pace with her.

"Don't you?" he repeated.

"I might."

"I'm going with you."

"You should stay here. You might be needed." Her voice shook a little on that. If Joey was hurt, she meant.

"I can be reached on the cell phone."

"I don't want—"

He caught her arm, turning her to face him, frustration and fear warring inside him. "Face facts, Maggie. I know you want to do everything by yourself, but you can't. If you do find him, you'll need someone along to help. Like it or not, I'm going with you."

He could see emotion surging beneath the surface, but she set her mouth and nodded. She jerked a nod toward the truck, and he scrambled in.

She whipped down the street, then turned onto the narrow back road they'd taken the day they'd gone to help the injured man back in the woods. The windshield wipers fought against the thick, wet snow— huge flakes that piled up swiftly and would hamper the search.

"Why do you think he came this way?" If he didn't pump her, he didn't think she'd say a word.

"We were out by my family's house one day in the fall. I pointed out the logging trail that went over the mountain." Her face lost a little more color, if possible.

"He'd know we'd look along the main road. I can't be sure, but it's worth a try."

Poor Maggie. She had something else to blame herself for. "You couldn't imagine these circumstances. It's not your fault."

"It's my responsibility."

The truck skidded as she took a bend too fast, and she fought the wheel. He grabbed it, helping her regain control.

"Take it easy. We can't help him if we smash ourselves up."

If she heard, she didn't acknowledge his words. She seemed to force the truck on by sheer willpower, barreling through the thickly piled snow. He braced his hand against the dash, sure they'd end up smashed against a tree, but she kept it going somehow.

If they didn't find Joey safe… He couldn't begin to see all the ramifications of that. Plenty of lives would be smashed then, that he knew.

The truck barreled along, its cab a warm cocoon protecting them from the storm. They reached the turnoff to the house where she'd once lived. The dilapidated mailbox still hung from its post, but the lane was drifted shut.

She hesitated, gunning the motor, and he grabbed her hand.

"Don't, Maggie. We'll need the truck usable if we find him. We'll have to walk in."

She held out against him for a moment, and then she nodded. "You're right."

She turned off the motor and slid out of the cab. He followed suit, slogging around the truck.

Maggie stared at the narrow lane. "What if I'm wrong? He may not be anywhere near here."

He spotted faint traces in the snow. "Look. The toboggan could have made those marks."

She looked doubtful. "It could have been an animal." She pulled out her cell phone, then shoved it back in her pocket. "We'd better find out for sure before we call people off any other area."

Nodding, he pulled his collar up and struck into the lane. He sank to above his knees at the first step. "It'll be slow going."

"I know." She was right behind him, her face set and determined.

He struggled on a few more arduous steps, apprehension growing. Maybe those had been animal tracks.

"How could he possibly have gotten through this? It's so deep, I can hardly make it."

"He could." Her voice was thick, as if with tears. "He's a strong little kid, and he had a head start on us. It wouldn't have been as deep an hour ago." She choked back a sob. "I have to believe that. I have to."

He reached out to grab her hand, pulling her through the deep drift. "I know." He sought for anything that would comfort her. "He's smart, too."

Maggie nodded, but her eyes were bleak, almost dead.

*She won't survive if we lose this child.* Who was

he talking to? The God he wasn't sure he believed in anymore? *You have to help.*

God hadn't saved Jason. What made him think He'd save Joey?

She had to pull herself together. She couldn't give in to her fear.

*Help us, Father. Help Joey. Your children need you so desperately today.*

Grant's hand gripped hers, pulling her along through the deepest of drifts. Maybe that was part of God's answer. She hadn't wanted Grant with her today. She would have come alone if she could have.

And that would have been wrong. She couldn't do this alone.

*Thank You. I wish Grant and I could at least be friends, but even if we can't, thank You for sending him with me today.*

"Wait." Breathless, she caught Grant's hand with both of hers. "There's the logging road." She nodded toward the cleft in the trees, barely perceptible in the thick snow.

He frowned. "Are you sure? It doesn't look like much."

"I'm sure." A shiver went through her, not entirely from the cold. She knew every inch of this terrain. "I don't see how he could have gone that way, not without leaving a trace."

Grant pointed down the lane toward the house. "There. Doesn't that look like the marks the toboggan would leave?"

She didn't want to go down that way. She had to. "It could be. Joey knows where the house is—what's left of it, anyway. He might have gone there for shelter."

Grant's fingers tightened on hers. She felt the reassurance of his grasp through her thick gloves, warming her.

He knew how she felt about the place. How could he not? Pointless, now, to try and disguise her fears or anything else from him.

*"They that wait upon the Lord shall renew their strength."* The promise from Isaiah echoed in her mind, and a fresh spurt of energy propelled her forward.

"Let's go."

Again Grant forged ahead, pushing his legs through the deepening snow. If not for the track he made breaking the snow, she might not have made it.

They struggled around the bend, and the house loomed ahead of them. Or maybe *loomed* wasn't the right word for something that was tumbling down into itself as if from the sheer weight of unhappiness it had seen.

"Joey!" She coughed a little on the intake of cold air. "Joey, are you here? Answer me!"

The snow seemed to muffle her call, and nothing else broke the silence.

"Joey Bascom!" Grant added his voice to hers. "Where are you?"

He looked at her, eyes questioning. "It doesn't look disturbed, and it definitely doesn't look safe. Maybe we're on the wrong track."

"No." Improbable as it was, a sense of certainty swept through her. "He's here. I know he's here."

"Maggie—"

She pushed forward, closer to the place she'd never wanted to see again. "We have to check. We can't come this far and just walk away."

He followed her, and she felt his doubts. Did he think she was clinging to straws?

He brushed past her, leaning forward to peer into a broken window. "The whole roof is down, Maggie. There's not much shelter."

"He's here." She scrambled forward to grab at what had been exposed by Grant's movement. "Look." She pulled the toboggan free of the snow.

In a moment Grant had pushed away the rotted door and climbed into the house. He reached back a hand for her.

"Here, but where? Joey!"

He wasn't saying the thing he feared. That Joey didn't answer because he couldn't. That they were too late.

"The root cellar." She shoved past him, heading for the old summer kitchen. "He could shelter there." She had, more times than she cared to remember.

She yanked at the door, then stumbled down the three steps, jerking the flashlight from her pocket. "Joey?"

"There." Grant jumped down the steps, rushed to the side wall where a whole section of shelves had fallen. Beneath the shelves—

"Joey!" She couldn't breathe as she stumbled across to him. He was so still, so white. *Father—*

Grant dropped to his knees, shoving the wooden shelves out of his way.

She dropped next to him, and she had to fight to hold the light steady on Joey's face. "Is he—"

Grant's hands moved swiftly and surely over the child's body. Then he looked up, and his smile blazed. "He's breathing."

"Thank God." Her tears spilled over, but she smiled back at him, feeling an instant of perfect harmony, perfect gratitude. "Thank God."

# Chapter Thirteen

Grant turned his attention firmly to the boy. That was the thing to do—think of him as any anonymous patient who'd been brought into the emergency room. Don't think of the little boy whose eyes had filled with wonder at the sight of that red toboggan. That way lay weakness, and he couldn't afford to be weak.

He cleared the debris carefully away from the child's shoulder and head. The arm lay at a bad angle.

"Looks like a dislocated elbow." He ran his hands along the boy's arms. "I don't think there's a break, but I'd like to see an X-ray."

Maggie was checking pulse and respiration. "Vitals look good. If he's been unconscious—"

She didn't finish that sentence, probably because at that moment Joey's eyelids flickered and opened.

"Maggie," he whispered. "Doc." He managed a smile. "I was asleep. I dreamed you came."

"Looks like your dream came true." Maggie touched his cheek gently. She sounded perfectly calm, as if they hadn't been hovering on the razor edge of disaster a few moments earlier.

"You'd better call this in." His voice was sharper than he intended it to be. "We'll need some help getting him out of here."

She sent him a questioning look, then nodded and moved toward the steps as she pulled out the cell phone. As he checked the child over carefully, he listened to the joy in her voice.

Maggie was happy. Resentment knifed its way into his thoughts. Had she forgotten so quickly why they were in this mess? If Jason—

He stopped, appalled at himself. This wasn't Jason. He looked at the boy, and for a moment the face in front of him wavered. It almost looked like his brother's face from so long ago.

*No.* What had made him think such a crazy thing? This was Joey.

Maggie came back, slipping the phone into her pocket. "They'll be here in a few minutes." She smiled at Joey. "We'll have you snug and warm in no time."

He touched the child's forehead. "I can't figure out why he's not colder than he is. He's been exposed to the weather for hours."

Joey wiggled a little. "It's not so cold in here. I remembered what Maggie said about the root cellar."

He glanced at her, lifting his eyebrows. "Root cellar?"

"We always kept vegetables in the root cellar in the winter. It's underground, so it stays at an even temperature. Joey was pretty smart to remember that."

"You were pretty smart to realize he might be here." He sat back on his heels, trying for a normal tone of voice. He wouldn't think about that moment when he'd confused Joey with his brother. Nor about his anger with her for getting them into this mess to begin with. He'd stay coolly professional.

Something changed in her face, just for a second. "I used to hide here."

Joey might think she meant as a game. He knew better. Maggie was talking about hiding from her father.

The images battered at him—Maggie cowering in a dirty corner. Maggie shivering, waiting for the door to burst open. He tried futilely to push the thoughts away. He seemed to have no emotional barricades left. He hated that.

The roar of a snowmobile motor broke the silence. Someone shouted from outside, and Maggie hurried up the steps.

"Here," she called. "We're here."

In moments the tiny cellar was filled to overflowing with people, pushing out all the ugly images.

"We brought the rescue truck, Doc." The barber/fire chief carried a litter down the steps. "We can put the litter on one of the snowmobiles to get him out to it."

He started to say they'd better carry the litter, and then remembered their struggle through the knee-deep snow to get here. The man was right. That would be safer.

"Good." He reached for the kit, but one of the

volunteers already had a neck collar ready to put in his hand. "We'll immobilize his neck and arm first."

It was reassuring to have familiar equipment at hand, comforting to go through the familiar movements. He could block out those moments when he'd seen his brother's face on Joey. When he'd seen a small Maggie cowering in the corner, weak and afraid.

In minutes they were ready to transport. Willing hands seized the litter and bore it gently to the waiting snowmobile. The motor purred. The driver moved off slowly and carefully with his precious cargo, several volunteers walking on either side.

He started to follow, but someone hustled him onto another waiting snowmobile. How had they all gotten here so quickly? The once-deserted area around the derelict house teemed with people, all trying to do something to help.

His snowmobile driver roared through the woods, apparently feeling no need to go slowly with him. He dismounted at the emergency truck and pulled open the rear door. Before he could do more than glance inside, another snowmobile roared to a stop next to him. Maggie got off, lifting her hand in thanks as the driver swung around.

"I want Joey taken straight to the nearest hospital," he said. "We'll ride with him."

Maggie shoved wet bangs out of her face. "That's not a good idea."

His jaw tightened until it felt as if it would break. As

usual, Maggie seemed to think she knew better than he did.

"This is no time to worry about someone finding out about the Bascoms."

She blinked. "That never entered my mind." She lifted her hands. "Look around. The snow hasn't let up—if anything, it's worse. The chopper won't fly in this, and the roads are bound to be bad. Jostling him along forty miles of slippery roads isn't going to help a dislocated elbow."

"He needs more sophisticated care than we can provide."

Was that the reason? What was wrong with him, that he'd let his professional judgment be hampered by this place and these people?

Maggie looked at him gravely, as if she knew what was going on beneath the surface.

She couldn't know. No one could.

The snowmobile with the litter pulled up. All he could see was Joey's small face as they lifted him into the van. Joey's face. Not Jason. Joey.

Maggie stepped closer. "Grant." She lowered her voice. "He really is better off at the clinic."

He didn't want this. He didn't have a choice. He gave a curt nod and climbed into the back of the van.

Maggie paused outside the clinic door a few hours later, taking a breath, lifting an almost wordless prayer. Joey had been treated with Grant's usual skill, and he was safely tucked up in bed with Aunt Elly in attendance and half the village running in and out bringing food or offering to watch the other children. Crisis over, she should be able to relax.

But she couldn't. Aside from every other worry, something was wrong with Grant. She'd felt his tension, so strong it vibrated through the room the entire time he'd taken care of Joey. Felt it, but not understood it.

*Help me, Lord. I don't know what's going on within Grant. Show me how to help him.*

She opened the door and went inside.

Grant stood at the desk, his head bent, hands braced on its surface. He'd changed into dry slacks and a gray sweater, and he should have looked warm, dry and relieved. He didn't.

*Please, Lord.*

"Joey's tucked into bed and nearly asleep. One more story from Aunt Elly should do it."

Grant turned his head to look at her, and the inimical expression in his eyes nearly stopped her heart.

"Why are you looking like that?" The question came out involuntarily. "He's all right. You should be happy."

"Happy?" His voice rose, and he took a step toward her. "I don't see much to be happy about in this situation."

"But he's all right," she repeated, not sure what else to say. Was he still worried that Joey needed more sophisticated care than they could provide? "You did everything they'd have done if we'd taken him to the hospital. He couldn't have received better care than you gave him."

"That's not the point. Don't you see that we can't be responsible for these children? Today should have made you face reality. Don't you realize that Jason could have died out there?"

For a moment she could only stare at him. "Joey. Not Jason." Then, as if a curtain had been pulled back, she knew. "Jason was your brother."

He looked gaunt suddenly, as if all the life and strength had been drawn out of him. "Joey. I meant Joey."

She'd asked God how to help him. Perhaps she was hearing the answer.

"Joey reminds you of your brother, doesn't he?"

"No." His mouth tightened. "They're totally different."

"Externally, maybe. But something about Joey still reminds you of him." She took a step, closing the gap between them, and put her hand on his arm. It felt like wood beneath her fingers. "Tell me, Grant. What happened to Jason?"

His face was so rigid it was a wonder he could move his lips. "He died. Childhood leukemia."

Her heart hurt for him. "I'm so sorry."

"That was a long time ago. It doesn't have anything to do with what's happening now."

"Maybe it shouldn't, but it does." A certainty that could only come from God pushed her on. "For some reason, you relate to Joey in the way you did to your brother. And you don't want to."

"No, I don't want to!" His reserve broke, so suddenly

that the wave of emotion nearly knocked her off balance. "I can't. I can't be a decent doctor if I let myself see Jason in every child I treat."

He tried to turn away, but she tightened her grasp, holding him. She couldn't let him retreat from this. Once he went back behind those protective barriers, he'd never come out again.

"You can't be a decent doctor if you're afraid to care."

"You sound like Dr. Rawlins. That was why he talked me into coming here. He thought I'd find some passion for my patients here." His hands clenched. "He thought Button Gap would make me open up. It's just shown me I was right all along."

"No." She wanted to shake him, as if that would make him see how painfully wrong he was. "You can't shut yourself off from people because you're afraid to lose them the way you lost your brother."

He whitened. She'd probably gone too far, but she couldn't stop now.

"You can't live that way, Grant." Her voice went soft, almost trembling with her need to reach him. "No one can."

His mouth curled in a mirthless smile. "Sure they can. My parents have been doing it for years."

"What do you mean?"

"My mother uses her social whirl, my father uses his business. They haven't felt a thing since the day we buried my brother."

She'd thought she already hurt as much as she could for him, but that revelation sliced into her heart. They hadn't felt a thing for him, the child they had left. "Who comforted you?" Not his parents, that was clear.

"I didn't need comforting. I don't need it now. I just need to—"

"What? Stop caring? Stop grieving? You can't shut other people out of your life."

He probably hadn't ever truly grieved for his loss. How could he, when his parents had blocked themselves off from caring? Her heart wept for him.

He shook her hand off, his face a mask of denied pain. "Leave it alone, Maggie. You're not exactly an advertisement for relying on other people yourself."

She felt as if he'd hit her. She caught her breath and fought to be honest, knowing only honesty could possibly reach him.

"Maybe so. I've been so determined not to be weak, like my mother was, that I couldn't accept help."

*Why couldn't you be strong, Mama? Why couldn't you protect me?* She struggled for control.

"Don't you see, Grant? That's something taking care of those kids made me face. I had to have help, and I got it. Button Gap didn't let me down—not when I was eleven, and not today."

"You belong here," he said stubbornly. "I don't. In a few more days, I won't have Button Gap. I'll be back in my real life."

"Back to helping people only when you can do it from a safe distance? Back to letting your white coat insulate you from caring?"

"That's my choice."

They'd come full circle. It *was* his choice.

"You're right." She clasped her hands to keep from reaching out to him. He didn't want her touch. "You can go straight back into that hard, cold shell of yours. It'll keep you safe from anything raw or painful. You can just go on blaming God."

A tiny muscle twitched in his jaw, the only sign a living human being existed behind the mask he wore. Maybe she'd probed the sorest spot of all.

"If God is there, He could have saved Jason." Implacable. He couldn't give an inch.

God alone knew the answer to that hard question. He knew, too, how much she'd struggled with it. Why did the innocent suffer? Maybe everyone had to deal with that one alone.

"God is there." Tears stung her eyes. "I don't know why your brother died, but I know God was there, holding him in His hands. I know God is ready to help you deal with it, if you'll let Him."

His face was closed and barred against her. "I don't want Him to. I don't need help. Not from Him. Not from you."

He grabbed his jacket and slammed his way out of the clinic. The door seemed to close on her heart.

She'd tried. She'd failed. Grant was lost to her for good. Worse, she was afraid he was lost to the only One who could help him.

By the time he stopped reacting and started thinking, Grant realized he'd walked to the edge of the village.

He hadn't bothered to zip his jacket, and the cold air seemed to permeate his very bones.

He zipped the jacket, pulling the collar up. He should go back. The snow had stopped falling, finally, but dusk was drawing in. This was no time to be out on a cold, lonely lane in the middle of nowhere.

He didn't want to go back. Didn't want to see anyone, speak to anyone. He particularly didn't want to see Maggie.

*Maggie.*

He shoved his fists into his pockets and looked up at the dark mountainside. His anger flared again, white-hot. How dare she say those things? She should be grateful to him instead of attacking him.

Maggie wouldn't see it as an attack, of course. She thought she was helping, as if taking a scalpel to his soul could possibly help him.

He'd spoken the truth, and she hadn't been able to take it. She couldn't accept the fact that he'd chosen to live his life cut off from God.

Maggie didn't understand. She didn't know what it was like, how he felt…

*Didn't she?*

Shame burned into him. Maggie was probably the only person who knew what he felt. She was certainly the only one he'd revealed anything to in years.

And Maggie couldn't be accused of having life easy. After what she'd gone through, how did she even manage to get up in the morning, let alone carve out a full, useful life for herself?

He knew the answer she'd give if he asked her the question. The one she called Father had brought her through it. She didn't see why the same didn't apply to him.

*Because I can't forgive You.*

The thought, coming from somewhere deep inside him, shocked him with its bone-deep honesty. Maybe he'd been kidding himself about a lot of things, but that, at least, was true. He hadn't forgiven God for taking Jason.

Those last days, with nurses taking over the house and running their lives—the images flooded in upon him. They hadn't let him see Jason. He'd curled miserably behind the drapes in the hall window seat, where he could watch the door to Jason's room, waiting for a chance to sneak in and see him.

The last day had been like this one—snow in the air, and the dusk drawing in early. Shadows had filled the hallway, as if they waited, too.

*Save him.* He'd gone beyond tears, beyond bargaining, beyond demanding. All his prayers had come down to those two words. *Save him.*

Now he glared up at the darkening sky, not sure whether he was the hurting boy or the grown man. *You took away the person who meant the most to me. What do You want from me now?*

There wasn't an answer now. Any more than there'd been an answer then.

Maybe it was better not to believe God existed. Then, at least, he'd have known there wasn't any hope.

The cold seeped through the soles of his boots, into his bones, into his soul. He turned, looking back toward Button Gap.

Lamps were on now, glowing warmly in windows. The strings of Christmas lights on the tree in front of the post office blinked red and green, and the stained-glass windows of the church gleamed like jewels against the white snow that blanketed the village.

Above, the mountains loomed dark and cold, but the first star made a pale point of light.

He exhaled, watching his breath form steam in the air. Still. Silent. Nothing moving, nothing speaking. Nothing touching him. He was as cold and isolated as the star.

Something floated toward him through the dusk. The notes of the piano, then the treble of children's voices.

"'Silent night, holy night, all is calm, all is bright...'"

It was Christmas Eve. The children were practicing for the pageant that would begin in another hour.

Maggie would be there, directing them and smiling as if nothing had happened. She probably expected him to walk in and take his place in the pew, pretending everything was normal.

He couldn't.

*You don't have to stay.* The thought formed without volition. *No one expects you to work out the week. You can pack and go. You never have to think of Button Gap and Maggie again.*

Even now he couldn't convince himself that he'd

dismiss Maggie from his thoughts so easily. But he could leave.

He started walking, his footsteps making little sound on the snow-packed lane. He'd pack and leave. He didn't have to go to his parents' house. He could hole up in a hotel somewhere until the holiday was safely over.

*You can go straight back into that hard, cold shell of yours.* He hadn't managed to get Maggie's voice out of his head yet. He'd have to try harder. *You can let your white coat insulate you from caring.*

*Leave me alone.* He didn't know if he was speaking to Maggie or to the God he wasn't sure he believed in. *Just leave me alone.*

## Chapter Fourteen

"'Bless all the dear children in Thy tender care, and fit us for heaven to live with Thee there.'"

The final notes of the old carol died away, and the children looked at Maggie expectantly.

"Wonderful." She managed to smile. "That's perfect. Just you sing it that way in the performance, and everyone will absolutely love it."

People were already filtering into the pews, talking softly so as not to disturb the rehearsal. They didn't mind that they'd see and hear the same thing again in half an hour. This was part of Christmas for them.

"Okay." She clapped her hands. "You can go and get your costumes on now. Mind, no running. I don't want any broken angel wings."

Released, the children scrambled off the chancel steps, toward the helpers who had costumes spread out over the pews. For a second she could breathe. She could think.

Maybe it would be better not to have time to think.

In only a moment of quiet, the pain surged back out of hiding, ready to sink sharp teeth into her again.

*"'And fit us for heaven, to live with Thee there.'"*

Grant's brother had lived those words the children sang so cheerfully. Surely God's hands had been around him, safe and comforting, in those last minutes.

Grant had been the one left alone and uncomforted. A fresh spasm of pain gripped her, tinged with guilt. She'd been so judgmental of him when they'd first met.

*Forgive me, Lord. You know how often I fall into that same sin. You must be tired of hearing me confess it.*

She'd thought she knew who Grant was—wealthy, privileged, taking his easy life for granted and perfectly willing to use a month in Button Gap to get something he wanted.

She hadn't been willing, or able, to look beneath the surface for the pain that lived there. She, of all people, should know how often a calm exterior could hide a raging grief. She'd been there most of her life, and her own shield had been hard-won.

She hadn't bothered to look for what Grant was hiding until life, in the form of the Bascom family, had forced both of them into sharing things they'd otherwise never have told each other. Now she knew him all the way through.

She understood his pain. And he wouldn't let her do one thing to help him with it.

She squeezed her eyes closed, shutting out the kaleidoscope of children, costumes, Christmas tree, chattering adults.

*Help him, Father. I can't. I wanted to, but he wouldn't let me. He's going away, and I can't do anything to make a difference.*

Cold certainty gripped her. Grant would go away. He might be on his way already.

*Please, Father. I've lost any chance I had.*

She struggled to see her way through the days ahead. She'd do what she had to do—try to help the Bascoms, try to keep the clinic running. She'd keep putting one foot in front of the other, and one day, unlikely as it seemed right now, she'd be happy again.

*Be with him, Lord. Hold him in Your hands.*

That felt like a benediction, but with it came some small measure of peace. She'd done everything she could. The rest was up to the Father.

Aunt Elly slipped an arm around her waist. "Are you okay, child?"

She took a shaky breath. She hadn't told Aunt Elly yet. She hadn't told anyone, but she'd have to. They wouldn't understand why Grant wasn't here for the pageant.

"I'm all right. But Grant—" Her throat closed.

Aunt Elly squeezed her. "He's fighting something, isn't he?"

She nodded. "I wanted to help. I'm afraid I just made things worse. He's probably packing to leave right now."

"Have you turned it over to God?"

Had she? Maggie searched for any reservation, any self-interest clouding her prayers for Grant.

"Yes," she said finally. "I have."

"That's all we can do, then." She pressed her cheek against Maggie's. "Have faith, Maggie. Maybe you planted the seed that will make a change in his life. We're not always called to see the harvest, you know. Just to be faithful in planting the seed."

Aunt Elly had certainly done that in her own life. Now it was up to Maggie to do the same.

"I know." Her smile felt more genuine. "Well, let's get those children dressed. What have you done with Joey?"

Aunt Elly pointed to the front pew. Joey, nestled in a pile of cushions, reclined like a sultan, his arm positioned carefully in its sling. He was a little pale, but he grinned when he saw her looking at him.

"You didn't think we'd be able to keep him away, did you? He says he's going to make sure the substitute king does it right."

She actually felt like laughing, something she'd thought it would take years to accomplish. "He'll probably scare the poor kid into making a mistake, more likely."

"It's going to be all right." Aunt Elly sounded sure of herself. "It always is."

"True enough." No matter what mistakes anyone made, the pageant still always announced its eternal truth to hearts willing to hear it. "I guess—"

She stopped, realizing that a hush had fallen over the sanctuary. The door swung to with a clatter.

She turned, looking toward the back of the sanctuary to see who had come in. Looked, identified and felt her heart freeze in response.

Mrs. Hadley, the county social worker, stood just inside the door. Gus Foster, looking harassed and reluctant but official in his deputy's uniform, stood beside her.

Mrs. Hadley didn't look harassed or reluctant. She looked triumphant.

The children—

From the corner of her eye, Maggie saw Evie Moore drop an angel gown over Tacey's head and sweep Robby behind her with a deft movement.

Brave, but futile. Maggie's mind scrambled for ways to get the children out, even as she recognized the impossibility of it all. Joey, immobilized in his nest of cushions, couldn't be hidden, and Mrs. Hadley's eagle eye had probably already identified the other two.

*Help.* She couldn't seem to manage anything else in the way of a prayer, and Mrs. Hadley was advancing down the center aisle like a Sherman tank, flattening anything and anyone that dared to be in its path. *Help!*

"Margaret Davis." The woman rumbled to a stop dead center. "I thought it would be you."

"Mrs. Hadley." It was a sign of recognition between enemies, as if flags dipped before a battle. "Have you come for the pageant?"

The woman swelled. "I've come for the Bascom children, as you well know. You've been hiding them from me."

Not from social services, Maggie noted, even as her mind ran this way and that, searching for a way out. For Mrs. Hadley, this was personal. Was the woman still trying to assert her authority over the rebellious eleven-year-old Maggie had once been?

"I don't know what you mean."

Maggie felt Pastor Jim move up next to her. She sensed the rest of Button Gap arranging itself behind her. It was a good sensation.

Unfortunately, that support wouldn't be enough. Mrs. Hadley had brought the law with her. Gus didn't want to be here—that was clear from his hangdog expression. He had better things to do with his Christmas Eve. But he'd do his duty, like it or not.

Mrs. Hadley's eyes were small and mean behind her wire-rimmed glasses. She hadn't changed, it seemed to Maggie, in the past two decades. She'd gotten a little grayer, a little meaner, a little fatter.

Maggie had once looked at her bulk and seen a mountain of a woman, terrifying in her power. The power was still there, but she wouldn't allow herself to be terrified any longer.

Mrs. Hadley sent a commanding glance toward Gus. He shifted uncomfortably and cleared his throat.

"We're here to pick up the Bascom kids." There was an apology in the look he gave Maggie. "Seems Mrs. Hadley's office has some information that Nella Bascom ran off and left those kids."

"Ran off?" Maggie raised her eyebrows, trying for a composure she didn't feel. "Just because Nella went on a trip doesn't mean she deserted her children."

"Certainly not." Pastor Jim waded in. "Nella left her

children in Maggie's care when she had to go away for a while. There's nothing wrong with that."

"That's what I've been saying." Gus looked relieved at the pastor's intervention, undoubtedly seeing it as a way out of a situation he disliked. "Nothing wrong with that."

"Nothing wrong?" Mrs. Hadley gave him a contemptuous look. "You'd take anything these people said as gospel and use it as an excuse not to do your duty."

Gus stiffened. "I don't need nobody telling me how to do my duty. If the woman deserted her kids, I'll help you take them in. But seems like we've got a dispute about that."

"Nella asked me to take care of her children while she was away. I said yes." Maggie hoped she sounded as if that would be an end to it.

"If that's the case, where is she?" Mrs. Hadley fired the question like a dart. "If you're taking care of her children for her, you must know where she is."

"She had to go back to West Virginia." She chose her words carefully. "She has family there."

"That's right," Aunt Elly chipped in. "We all know Nella's family's from West Virginia."

Mrs. Hadley dipped into her bag and pulled out a cell phone. She held it out to Maggie with a malicious gleam in her eyes. "Then you know how to reach her. Call her, now. If she tells me what you're saying is true, I'll leave it alone. For the moment."

There was the challenge. Mrs. Hadley would only make it if she felt sure Maggie couldn't do just that.

And she couldn't. *Oh, Nella. Why didn't you trust me enough to tell me where you are?*

The cell phone waved in the air between them. Mrs. Hadley's air of triumph grew. Her tongue snaked out to moisten her lips, as if she tasted victory.

"Take it." Aunt Elly's voice was soft in her ear. "Call Grant. We need him."

Just the sound of his name was an arrow in her heart. *We don't,* she wanted to say. *We don't need him. He walked away from us. He's leaving.*

Is that really the reason? The question dropped quietly into her mind. Is that the reason, or is it because you don't want to admit you need him?

Her instant response told her the truth. Grant didn't need her. She didn't want to need him. She couldn't rely on him.

But she had to.

Grant slammed the back of the SUV on all the belongings he'd brought with him to Button Gap. He was ready to go. There was nothing to keep him here any longer.

He glanced toward the church. It must be time for the pageant to start. Maybe it was already under way. All of Button Gap would be gathered there. He was the only holdout.

Well, he wasn't part of Button Gap. He never had been.

His cell phone rang, a shrill, imperative summons. For an instant he was tempted to ignore it. He couldn't.

He snapped the phone open. "Hardesty."

"Mrs. Hadley is here." Maggie's voice was a whisper—a frightened whisper. "Come to the church. Please. We need you." A slight hesitation. "I need you."

"Maggie?"

The connection was broken.

He stared at the phone, then turned to stare at the church. Mrs. Hadley was there. Maggie needed him.

He could slide behind the wheel and drive away. He didn't have to be involved in this. The roof was falling in on Maggie's scheme, and all he had to do was drive away.

He couldn't, any more than he'd been able to ignore the call. He couldn't shut Button Gap out of his life, like it or not. Not yet.

He jogged across the street toward the church. Maggie had called him. Maggie had asked for his help.

That was the strangest thing. Maggie—determined, fiercely independent Maggie—wanted his help. She'd actually put away her pride and asked for help.

Could he give it? He paused at the foot of the church steps, gripping the railing.

He'd told himself all along that calling social services would be best for those children. He'd let himself be manipulated into the conspiracy to hide them, knowing all along that he shouldn't.

Now it had been taken out of his hands—out of all their hands. Mrs. Hadley was there. Presumably she knew about the Bascom kids. What should he do, even if he could?

*Isn't this for the best?* With a sense of shock, he realized he was speaking to the God he'd been trying so hard to ignore. *Isn't turning those kids over the right thing? They're not my responsibility.*

*Why not?* The voice seemed to whisper in his heart. *Why aren't they your responsibility?*

*Because when I looked at Joey, hurt and helpless, all I could see was my brother. I can't take responsibility for them, don't You see that? What do You want from me?*

*All of you.* The answer rang through him. *All of you. Not just your skill as a doctor. All of you.*

He bent over, his breath coming as if he'd been running. The cold air seared his lungs. He couldn't. He couldn't give in, couldn't trust. He'd trusted God with Jason, and look what had happened.

*Jason is safe in God's hands.* That was what Maggie's message had been, and the words resounded, refusing to leave him alone.

If that was true, how could he go on using his brother as a reason not to take responsibility for another child?

He straightened slowly, looking at the church door, feeling its pull. Quickly, without letting himself think of possible consequences, he ran up the steps, pulled the door open and ran inside.

## Chapter Fifteen

Grant stepped inside the sanctuary and paused, assessing the situation. The pews of the small church were filled with people. All of Button Gap had come to spend Christmas Eve watching the children's pageant.

Instead, they were seeing a pageant of a different sort.

Maggie stood at the front of the sanctuary, the deep red of her sweater making the pallor of her face more pronounced. Pastor Jim, next to her, had distress written across his countenance.

The woman opposite them looked ready to take on all comers, hands planted on her hips, brows drawn down, eyes glinting behind her glasses. Next to her, the deputy sheriff he'd met before stood representing the law, no matter how reluctantly. The battle lines were drawn.

For a moment it seemed to Grant an epic battle between good and evil. He shook off that fancy and started down the aisle at a deliberate pace. No one here was evil. They were just people trying to do what they thought was right. Maybe that was even more frightening.

*Take it slow and easy,* he told himself, aware that most of the people in the sanctuary were watching him now, as if a new fighter had entered the arena. Knowing Maggie's penchant for charging into situations, this one had probably already escalated too fast, too far.

The best thing he could do was calm the rhetoric and get some sort of delaying movement. Maggie had turned this woman into a monster in her mind, but surely any social worker worth her salt couldn't really want to take the children away on Christmas Eve.

Maggie, confronting the woman she considered her enemy, looked as strong and determined as a crusader ready to die for her cause. Then she glanced toward him, and he saw the pleading in her eyes.

He faltered, almost losing his place in the open pain of that look. Maggie needed him.

Mrs. Hadley, apparently alerted to his presence by the shifting of attention in her audience, swung ponderously to face him, too.

"Grant." Maggie's voice was strained, held calm, he was sure, by sheer effort. "This is Mrs. Hadley."

Then, apparently realizing she should have done it the other way around, she blinked. "This is Dr. Grant Hardesty, the physician who's working at the clinic this month."

He nodded, sizing the woman up. Solid, entrenched, sure of herself—she reminded him of a parade of bureaucrats he'd dealt with in his professional life. He didn't detect any of the fierce passion for the underdog he'd seen in other children's advocates.

All of that passion came from Maggie. Mrs. Hadley stood secure in her authority and her rules and regulations. She wouldn't back down easily.

"I don't know why you wanted to call him." Mrs. Hadley dismissed him with a glance. "The only thing that matters is that you don't know how to reach those children's mother. That gives me every right to put them in foster care." She swung on the deputy. "Do your duty, for once in your life."

"Just a moment." Grant's words, quietly spoken, had enough steel to bring a quick appraising look from the deputy. "I'd like to know what's going on here."

"What interest is it of yours?" Mrs. Hadley snapped.

The question, rude as it was, went right to the heart of the situation. If he admitted his involvement, that would spell even more trouble for the clinic, probably dooming his chance at the partnership. To his astonishment, that didn't mean as much as it had just a day ago.

*All of you.* The words echoed in his mind. *I want all of you.*

He'd been so sure that his future was his own to determine. Admitting that it wasn't brought an amazing sense of freedom, and with that feeling came the knowledge of how to play this situation.

He swung on Maggie. "Well, Ms. Davis, what's going on? Perhaps you'll be good enough to explain."

Pain flashed in her eyes at his curt tone. Then she seemed to recognize the incongruity of his question.

Her eyes widened. Her lips twitched, as if she held back an unguarded remark. Then she turned away, her hair swinging down to hide her face.

"I don't know what Mrs. Hadley is doing here." She managed to produce a sulky tone that was a perfect counterpoint to his arrogant doctor routine.

He should have known she'd instantly grasp what he wanted. After all, wasn't that how they'd worked together through every crisis of the past month?

"Try to explain," he said condescendingly.

He sent a covert glance toward the social worker. Her faint smile suggested that she liked hearing him put Maggie down. He had to control an anger that was surely irrational, since that was just the reaction he wanted.

"She seems to think Nella Bascom has deserted her children. We've tried to explain that we're just taking care of them while she's away, but Mrs. Hadley won't listen."

He paused for a beat, then turned toward the woman, raising his eyebrows. "I think that's perfectly clear. What seems to be the problem?"

Mrs. Hadley's face tightened until she looked like an angry bulldog. "It's a nest of lies, that's what's wrong. Those children belong under my supervision."

"I can't imagine why you feel that's necessary. They've been under the care of a physician and a nurse, not to mention the minister and half the town." He paused, letting that sink in. "Why would we need you?"

There was an approving stir in the congregation. Someone said a resounding Amen.

Mrs. Hadley's face flushed. "No one here knows where Nella Bascom is. You can't deny that. I gave Maggie a chance to call her, and she couldn't do it."

"Naturally not." Please, let this be true. "How can anyone reach her when Nella is en route to Button Gap for Christmas?"

"You expect me to believe that?"

He shrugged. "It's immaterial to me what you believe."

An approving flicker in Gus's face alerted him. The deputy, he'd guess, might weigh in on their side if he could give him a reason.

"The fact is, it's Christmas Eve," he continued. "Even if you had a reason for suspecting someone was breaking the law, I can't imagine any good social worker would try to snatch children away from a safe situation on Christmas Eve."

"I knew I'd find them in church on Christmas Eve if they were here." Her arrogance was tinged, for the first time, with defensiveness.

He raised his eyebrows. "Really." Two syllables to express doubt. "That hardly seems a reason to me for such drastic action."

"That's what I've been saying right along," Gus said. "We ought to let this go till after Christmas."

The woman's flush deepened alarmingly. "I didn't ask for your opinion."

Gus hesitated, probably weighing his desire to go home to his family against the Hadley woman's political clout. He needed something to push him over the edge.

Grant pulled out his cell phone. "Something was mentioned about calling Nella Bascom," he said pleasantly. "I'm afraid I can't do that, but my speed dial does connect with the home phone of John Gilbert, senior partner in Gilbert, Gilbert and Hayes. He handles the legal affairs of the Hardesty Foundation. I'm sure he wouldn't mind disturbing—" He paused, turning to Gus. "By the way, who's the county judge?"

Gus grinned. "That would be Layton Warren."

"I'm sure my attorney wouldn't mind calling Judge Warren on Christmas Eve, if necessary, to obtain an injunction preventing you from removing the children pending a hearing." He raised the phone. "Shall I make the call?"

The sanctuary was hushed. It felt as if no one so much as took a breath. He sensed, quite suddenly, the wave of prayer flooding the room from all those souls sending up the same petition at one time.

Mrs. Hadley was as pale now as she'd been ruddy before. Her mouth moved twice. Then she spoke.

"That won't be necessary," she said in a strangled tone.

"No, indeed," Gus said promptly, taking her arm in a firm grip.

Grant could breathe, but he couldn't relax yet. "I'm glad we're in agreement. I'm sure none of us wants further unpleasantness." Grant dropped the phone back into his pocket.

"Guess we've held up the Christmas pageant long enough." Gus nudged the woman toward the door.

For a moment Grant thought she'd stage a comeback. Then she seemed to sag into herself. She allowed the deputy to propel her to the door.

Gus paused, touching the brim of his hat. "Merry Christmas, folks."

Grant caught the sound of Maggie's sigh of relief, so soft no one else could have heard it. He wanted to turn to her, sharing the moment.

But even if they hadn't stood in full view of the entire village, that probably wasn't a good idea. His own emotions ran too high, and he could only imagine what she might be feeling.

They'd saved the Bascom kids for the moment, but nothing was resolved between them. That was the bottom line.

He'd better be perfectly sure he knew what he wanted before he said one more word to her.

There'd been a moment when she might have said something to Grant—tried to express her feelings. Then the organ started to play, the children filed into their places and the opportunity had passed. Maggie, kneeling next to the front pew, motioned the shepherds to close their eyes in feigned sleep before the angels startled them awake.

God, breaking into ordinary lives and making them different. Making them new.

Was that what was happening to Grant? She couldn't think of anything else to account for the extraordinary change in his attitude.

Grant, the person who'd pushed all along to turn the children over to social services, had instead walked into the sanctuary and taken on the system he'd claimed to rely upon.

Walked in? Maybe that wasn't quite the right explanation for Grant's appearance.

The angels popped out from behind the chancel rail, waking the shepherds. Mary Jo Carter's blue jeans peeked from the hem of her white gown, adding an interesting contrast to her angel costume. Someone should have caught that before the performance started. Her, probably. But she'd been a bit preoccupied, hadn't she?

She'd called Grant. In that moment of crisis, when she'd faced something she couldn't handle on her own, she'd called on him for help.

Maybe that wasn't as surprising as she thought. Maybe she'd been moving in that direction throughout the past month, as their lives had become more and more entwined.

He'd come—that was the significant thing. He'd answered her cry for help, and he'd saved them.

She had no illusions about that. If Grant hadn't appeared just when he did, the Bascom kids would be on their way to spending Christmas Eve in foster care. No one else would have succeeded in stopping Mrs. Hadley. He'd thrown his power and influence into the mix, and that had swung the balance to their side.

What was it going to cost him?

The organist hit the opening chords of "The First

Noel," and the congregation rose to join the children in the carol. Under cover of the movement, she glanced back to the center aisle.

Halfway back, Grant shared a hymnal with Aunt Elly. He could have left. He could have walked right out the door behind Gus and Mrs. Hadley, but he hadn't. She wasn't sure what that meant.

He'd been willing to risk the partnership he wanted for the sake of the children. He could still lose, and so could they. If Nella didn't come back, Mrs. Hadley would undoubtedly be seeing the judge the day after Christmas. The resulting clash might end with the clinic closed and Grant's partnership destroyed.

Why had he taken that chance?

*Not because of me, Lord. I know that. Have You found a way into his heart?*

The shepherds, sneakers showing beneath their robes, had found their way into the stable to kneel before the manger. The sheep, provided by Dawson Carter from his flock, gazed at them benignly. Her throat tightened.

These people—her people—probably understood as much as anyone about this familiar scene. They lived close to the land, too. They knew what it was to stand in a barn on a cold winter's night and feel the warm breath of the animals, patient in their stalls.

The kings, surprisingly stately in their makeshift finery, moved toward the manger. Their presence pricked her.

God had not kept His revelation only for the poor

and humble. The rich and powerful had been invited to that stable, too.

She glanced at Joey, half expecting tears, but he watched the kings with a critical eye, apparently ready to pounce on any mistake.

The pageant moved to its timeless conclusion, and the organ sounded the final carol. As always, it was "Away in a Manger." The children's voices piped in the first chorus, and her tears spilled over. She let them fall, unashamed.

As the congregation joined in the second verse, she looked again toward Grant. He sang with the rest, and his eyes shone with tears.

*Has he resolved his quarrel with You, Father? Has he found his way through his grief?*

If he had, then Grant was whole again. She couldn't ask for more than that.

She couldn't, no matter how much she wanted to. She'd never really believed there could be anything serious between them, but she'd gone and fallen in love with him anyway.

Well, she'd deal with it. He'd go back to Baltimore, and she'd deal with that, too. Knowing him, loving him, had helped her move past some of her private demons. She'd be a better Christian for having loved him.

Her gaze drifted over the faces of her friends—no, her family. She loved them. They loved her. With all their faults, they'd never let her down. They never would.

Someone moved, drawing her attention to the very rear of the sanctuary. Her breath caught in her throat. Nella. Nella had come home for Christmas.

## Chapter Sixteen

Maggie's heart was so full she couldn't speak a word. She could only watch as others realized Nella was there. A wave of joy seemed to pulse through the sanctuary, uniting them.

Willing hands pushed Nella toward the front, with people patting her, hugging her.

Maggie grabbed Tacey, who was nearest to her. "Look." She pointed. "Look who's here."

Nella stepped clear of the crowd. Tacey and Robby were a blur of movement as they rushed into her arms.

Maggie started toward Joey, but Grant reached him first. He scooped the boy up and carried him to his mother.

Following them, Maggie saw the expression on Grant's face as he put Joey into Nella's arms. The guarded look had vanished from his eyes. Anyone who looked could see the loving person Grant was inside, and he didn't seem to care.

*Thank You, Father.* Somehow the thought that he

would leave didn't hurt quite as much, because she could see beyond her own personal pain. *You used us to reach him. No matter what he does or where he goes, he'll be a better person and a better doctor for having been here.*

"Maggie." Nella reached out to embrace her, squishing Tacey between them in a joyful hug. "Thank you. Thank you."

She looked tired and thin, but her hazel eyes shone with a peace that transcended the external. Nella looked like a person who'd been through fire and come out with a new sense of who she was.

"We're glad you're home." Maggie gestured toward Grant. "This is Dr. Hardesty."

"I already told her," Joey said importantly. "I told her how Dr. Grant took care of me."

"I'd heard about the doctor. My aunt told me you folks came all the way to West Virginia looking for me."

Maggie shook her head, remembering the elderly woman who'd shut the door in her face. "She did a good job of telling us she'd never heard of you."

"I was worried." A flush rose in Nella's pale cheeks. "Guess about now I'm feeling pretty ashamed of how I acted. I don't know why you went on trusting me."

"Because we knew you'd do the right thing." Maggie squeezed her.

Nella wiped away a tear. "I figured I wasn't a very strong person. But knowing you—" Her glance seemed to gather in the whole village, pressing around her. "Knowing all of you had faith in me, well, I guess that convinced me I should have faith in myself."

"You have friends here," Pastor Jim said. "We won't let you down."

"Probably Mrs. Hadley would still say I can't make it, if I have to depend on other people."

"Mrs. Hadley isn't human enough to understand." Maggie realized she could think of the woman now without her childhood fear. "We all need help sometimes." Did Grant understand what she was saying? "Sometimes we just have to learn how to ask for it."

Nella's smile trembled on the verge of tears. "I won't be the person I was in my marriage. Not ever again."

For an instant Maggie seemed to see her mother's face, and the last faint bitterness slipped from her heart.

*She did the best she could, Father. I see that now. Thank You that Nella found herself before it was too late for her and the children.*

"Thank you, all of you." Nella's whisper seemed to penetrate the farthest reaches of the sanctuary. "God bless you."

Pastor Jim cleared his throat. "That sounds like a benediction to me. God bless us all. And now—" his smile broke through "—I happen to know that a birthday cake for Jesus is waiting downstairs. Let's celebrate."

Maggie was caught in a flood of goodwill as people moved toward the stairs. As she reached the last pew, Grant caught her arm.

"Come outside with me for a minute, Maggie." His eyes were very serious. "I have something to say to you."

*Goodbye.*

The word pierced her heart. Grant's time in Button Gap had come to an end. He wanted to say goodbye.

She wanted to run downstairs, hide in the crowd and pretend this wasn't happening. But she wouldn't be a coward about it.

She nodded, and they stepped together out into the starlit, silent night.

How did he say what he needed to say to Maggie? His heart was so full he felt as if he'd choke when he tried to speak.

They walked down the few steps to the sidewalk. Button Gap lay still around them, its lights flickering bravely against the blackness of the mountains looming above.

Maggie's head was tipped back, and he realized she looked, not at the mountains, but at the sky. It was a paler gray, spread with the crystal light of countless stars. The village's Christmas lights were a simple imitation of the real thing.

"Do you ever wonder what it was really like?" Maggie's murmur barely touched the silence.

"I know," he said as softly. "It was like this. Dark, quiet, seeming lonely, but filled with good-hearted people who are open to miracles."

"You see that now?" She made it a question.

He turned, so that they stood facing each other. He wanted to take her hands, but wasn't sure he should. Not yet.

"Yes." He took a breath, trying to find the words.

"You know what I was doing before I came here. I was trying to deny God's existence, as if that would make my grief easier to control."

"That doesn't work." Her voice was gentle. "I know. I tried. You can't box up pain and pretend it's not there."

"I might never have faced that if I hadn't come here." He looked inward, probing for the truth. "Jason knew God was with him every step of the way." He had to smile in spite of himself. "He's probably been bugging God ever since, wanting to know when He planned to make me recognize the truth. That was Jason."

It was the first time he'd been able to say Jason's name without pain—the first time he could smile in remembrance. Suddenly memories flooded through him in a tidal wave. Happy memories—things he'd locked away with the pain of Jason's death.

"As long as I couldn't deal with Jason's death, I couldn't remember his life." He did reach for her hands then. Hers were cold, but warmed to his touch. "You've given him back to me, Maggie."

"Not me. The Father did." Starlight reflected in her eyes. "He used me, and I wasn't a very willing tool."

"You can think of Him as Father, in spite of what your own father did."

"Aunt Elly helped me see that I could either let my past destroy me or I could let God use it to make me stronger. Seeing Him as a true Father was a big step forward for me."

She had a way of putting matters of faith into the simplest of terms. Once he'd have thought that naive, but no longer. Now he understood the strength and power of that.

"I almost let Jason's death destroy who I could be. I thought I was handling things better than my parents, because all they could do was give money in his memory. I thought giving my talent to healing was enough."

"But it wasn't."

She deserved to hear all of it.

"No. It's not enough. I realized tonight that God doesn't want the little pieces of me I've been willing to give. He wants all of me." He took a breath, letting the certainty settle deep inside him. "So that's what He's getting."

Joy lit Maggie's face, and her hands gripped his. "I'm glad. You'll be a better doctor for it, I promise you. When you go back—"

"I'm not going back."

Maggie's eyes widened. "Your partnership—surely that won't be a problem now. You can explain."

"I don't want to explain. I want to stay here." He smiled. "I might not be the doctor you'd have chosen for Button Gap, but I think I'm the one Someone Else picked."

"You can't give up everything you've wanted professionally."

"Maggie, listen. It's not giving something up when you've found something you want more. I want to be here. I want to be an important part of people's lives in a way I never could somewhere else. Button Gap needs me, but I need Button Gap just as much. It makes me whole."

Hope battled doubt in her expressive face. "The county can't afford a full-time doctor. It's been hard enough to get them to fund the clinic."

He smiled. "Oddly enough, I don't need the county's salary. As a matter of fact, I think I can convince the family foundation to provide us with a better facility. They like giving away money."

"You'd actually do that? You won't be sorry sometime down the road?"

He knew the answer to that one. "I'll never be sorry. This is what I want."

The church bells began to chime. Maggie looked up at the starry sky, as if hearing their echo in the stars.

"It's midnight. Merry Christmas, Grant."

He reached into his jacket pocket for the gift he'd been carrying around all day. He held it out to her.

"Merry Christmas, Maggie."

The crystal angel dangled from his fingers, glinting with reflected starlight.

He heard the sudden intake of her breath. She took the angel in both hands, and tears shone in her eyes. "It's beautiful."

It was time to say the rest of it, and he was absurdly afraid she might not give him the answer he longed for.

"I love you, Maggie Davis. Will you be my partner and my wife?"

The bells fell silent, as if the world waited with him

for her answer. Then he heard the voices ringing out from the church. "'Joy to the world, the Lord is come…'"

Maggie's face reflected that joy as she stepped forward into his arms. "I love you."

His lips claimed hers, and his heart filled with the certainty that he'd finally found his way home for Christmas.

*Epilogue*

"Let's put the angel toward the top of the tree." Standing on a step stool, he smiled down at Maggie. "Just to be on the safe side."

She glanced at the table, where Nella and Aunt Elly were helping the children string cranberries and popcorn together. "Good idea." She held the crystal angel up to him with a small, private smile. "I want this one to stay whole."

"Right." It had been a year since he'd given Maggie the new angel—a year of changes beyond measure in all their lives. He put the angel carefully on one of the topmost branches and watched it reflect the tree lights.

"I could come up and help you."

"Absolutely not." He stepped down from the stool and put one arm around her, then gently stroked the smooth, round curve that was just beginning to show. "I don't want little Jason or Emily to take any tumbles."

Maggie leaned against him and put her hand over

his. "The baby is fine. Leave it to a doctor to worry ten times as much as a normal father."

*Changes,* he thought again. Beautiful, blessed changes for all of them.

"Aunt Maggie, can I pat the baby, please?" Tacey danced over to them, her small face flushed with the excitement that only Christmas could bring.

"Sure you can." Maggie made room for the small hand.

Tacey wasn't withdrawn any longer, and Robby no longer looked around in apprehension when he laughed. As for Joey—he'd zoomed to the top of his class in school, determined to become a doctor, just like the person he now called "Uncle Grant."

With the completion of the new clinic, thanks to the Hardesty Foundation, the old building had been remodeled into two comfortable homes. Nella, proud of her position as the clinic office manager, lived with her children on one side, while he and Maggie would bring their new baby home to the other.

Maggie nestled her head against his shoulder as she looked at the nearly finished Christmas tree. "It's beautiful, isn't it?"

He dropped a kiss on her cheek. "It's beautiful. Just like everything else in my life now."

"Really?" She smiled at him teasingly. "You mean you like taking care of the whole county practically single-handedly? Taking payment in jars of jelly and cuts of venison? Crawling out of your warm bed to deliver a baby in the middle of a cold winter's night?"

He cradled her cheek in his palm, wondering at the love that seemed to grow stronger every day.

"I love every bit of it. Even the venison." He bent his head, his words for her alone. "God gave me everything I ever wanted when He brought me to Button Gap. He brought me home."

\* \* \* \* \*

Dear Reader,

I'm so glad you've chosen to read this book, and I hope the story touches your heart. Writing about Grant and Maggie's crusade to save the Bascom children made me smile and cry, and I hope you'll feel the same.

I know many wonderful children's services workers, and I hope they'll forgive me for making a social worker the villain in this particular story! My prayers are with all those who spend their lives protecting the Father's smallest children.

Please write me at Steeple Hill Books, 233 Broadway, Suite 1001, New York, NY 10279, and I'll be happy to send you a signed bookplate or bookmark. You can visit me on the web at www.martaperry.com or email me at marta@martaperry.com.

Blessings,

*Marta Perry*

# REQUEST YOUR FREE BOOKS!

## 2 FREE INSPIRATIONAL NOVELS
## PLUS 2
## FREE
## MYSTERY GIFTS

*Love Inspired*

---

**YES!** Please send me 2 FREE Love Inspired® novels and my 2 FREE mystery gifts (gifts are worth about $10). After receiving them, if I don't wish to receive any more books, I can return the shipping statement marked "cancel." If I don't cancel, I will receive 6 brand-new novels every month and be billed just $4.49 per book in the U.S. or $4.99 per book in Canada. That's a savings of at least 22% off the cover price. It's quite a bargain! Shipping and handling is just 50¢ per book in the U.S. and 75¢ per book in Canada.* I understand that accepting the 2 free books and gifts places me under no obligation to buy anything. I can always return a shipment and cancel at any time. Even if I never buy another book, the two free books and gifts are mine to keep forever.

105/305 IDN FVW5

Name                   (PLEASE PRINT)

Address                                         Apt. #

City                 State/Prov.                 Zip/Postal Code

Signature (if under 18, a parent or guardian must sign)

### Mail to the **Reader Service:**
**IN U.S.A.:** P.O. Box 1867, Buffalo, NY 14240-1867
**IN CANADA:** P.O. Box 609, Fort Erie, Ontario L2A 5X3

**Are you a subscriber to Love Inspired books
and want to receive the larger-print edition?
Call 1-800-873-8635 or visit www.ReaderService.com.**

\* Terms and prices subject to change without notice. Prices do not include applicable taxes. Sales tax applicable in N.Y. Canadian residents will be charged applicable taxes. Offer not valid in Quebec. This offer is limited to one order per household. Not valid for current subscribers to Love Inspired books. All orders subject to credit approval. Credit or debit balances in a customer's account(s) may be offset by any other outstanding balance owed by or to the customer. Please allow 4 to 6 weeks for delivery. Offer available while quantities last.

**Your Privacy**—The Reader Service is committed to protecting your privacy. Our Privacy Policy is available online at www.ReaderService.com or upon request from the Reader Service.

We make a portion of our mailing list available to reputable third parties that offer products we believe may interest you. If you prefer that we not exchange your name with third parties, or if you wish to clarify or modify your communication preferences, please visit us at www.ReaderService.com/consumerschoice or write to us at Reader Service Preference Service, P.O. Box 9062, Buffalo, NY 14269. Include your complete name and address.

LIDIR12

# LARGER-PRINT BOOKS!

**GET 2 FREE
LARGER-PRINT NOVELS
PLUS 2 FREE
MYSTERY GIFTS**

*Love Inspired*

*Larger-print novels are now available...*

LILPDIR12